WHEN A
Heartless
THUG
HOLDS ME CLOSE

A NOVEL BY

TYA MARIE

Yara

Sometimes you really have to ask if love is really enough. If being smiled to and fed the sweetest lies were worse than receiving a mouthful of the ugliest truth. I wasn't too sure it was, because no matter how many times I came home and leaned against my bedroom door, listening to my fiancé and best friend fuck each other's brains out, I always thought about what confronting them would do.

"You should go in there," I said to myself, taking a sip of my glass of wine, my hand shaking as I brought it to my face. "Go in there and fuck shit up. Remind him of the promises he made to you. The forever you're supposed to spend together."

I wasn't worried about them hearing me; they hadn't the entire month I had been coming home early from work to listen and play this guessing game. Every time I walked in the house and heard them fucking to the sounds of Tory Lanez or Bryson Tiller, I knew today would be the day. I went from sitting on the couch, praying for one of them to catch me sitting there, to leaning against the counter with my eyes closed wishing they would see me. Somehow I ended up at the door today, and each thud of the headboard rattled our vacation pictures hanging proudly on the wall.

"Right there, Amir," Sharise moaned. "Keep doing it right there, Daddy."

"Whose pussy is this?"

"It's yours."

I nearly choked on my wine; I had never heard them talk before. Yes, I knew they were sleeping with each other, but I had never heard Amir speak with such...passion. The inferno he brought to the bedroom with Sharise was nothing but a half lit match when it came to me. We made love, and it was beautiful, but this? This was a side that Amir had been hiding from me, amongst other things. I could tell him as much by busting this bedroom door open and confronting him, but was I ready for all of that?

I wasn't.

I made a mad dash for the front door as they came together, wrenching it open as quietly as I could and flinging myself out before they could hear the sob that escaped my lips. I closed the door just as quietly and ran as fast as I could through my apartment complex, my tears blurring my vision. I thought I saw my neighbor, Raz, as he brought his daughter home from school. *Shit*, I thought as I jogged through the slim walkway to my car, *everyone's getting home*. I ran into another one of my neighbors, Ms. Anna, with her middle-aged daughter, Anika, carrying bags. Ms. Anna looked confused as I brushed past her with a quick "hello," but judging by the way Anika was staring at me, she knew. I wondered who else knew the truth.

"Poor thing," I heard Ms. Anna say to Anika as I made it around the corner to the parking lot. "It was only a matter of time she found out."

I threw myself into my car, refusing to hear the rest of their conversation. Once I was behind the wheel, I let out the tears I had been desperately holding in. This wasn't how my life was supposed to go. I promised myself that when I found the one we would live happily ever—

"Hmm?" I said, glancing down at my cellphone buzzing in the cup holder next to me. I peeked at the ID and groaned, "Fuck."

It was Amir, and if I was louder than I thought, he probably heard me leaving out the house. I took three deep breaths, wiped my eyes, and picked up the phone.

"Hey, babe," I said casually, placing a hand over my mouth to keep any sobs from spontaneously erupting. "What's up?"

"Where you at?"

"On my way home from work. I had to stay a little longer because the other assistant manager was late. Why, you needed something?"

"Yeah, I was wondering if you could make lasagna tonight?" Amir said casually, like he hadn't finished getting all up in my best friend's guts. "I'm fiending for your lasagna."

"Yeah, I'll stop at the supermarket and grab the stuff to make it. Any more requests?"

"Nah," he said, and added as a second thought, "Your homegirl just showed up."

Deep breath. "Which one?"

"Sharise hoe ass. I told her you wasn't here so there was no need for her to be here, but you know how that bitch is. She doesn't know anything about boundaries."

"Damn sure don't," I co-signed, the words flying out of my moth before I could stop them.

Amir laughed. "I told you she ain't your friend."

"You know what…you might be right about that. I'll see you in a little while, babe."

"Love you."

Deep breath.

"Love you, too, Amir," I choked out, and hung up the phone.

I leaned my head against the headrest, shaking it from side-to-side to wake me from this dream where I became a weak woman indebted to a man. In all my years of living, I never thought I would've turned into my mother, allowing a man to control my life. I was amazing before Amir and I got together, and I was positive I would be amazing after, but the familiarity of our entire relationship had me thinking maybe I could spice things up. Nope, there was no way I could give up on us that easily. I would win my man back by doing whatever was necessary.

******

Cashmere stood in front of Victoria's Secret sipping on a smoothie from Jamba Juice, studying everyone that walked down the busy 34th Street intersection. She was dressed in the best from head-to-toe, a Moschino ensemble with a pair of Saint Laurent boots, her eyes hidden behind a pair of round Gucci frames. She slipped her shades off when she saw me, closing them with one hand and securing them in her

Chanel LeBoy bag. While she might have been dressed from head-to-toe in designer gear, Cashmere was as humble as they came. She was unfazed by my H&M chinos with a matching white blouse. I wasn't big on tags, and Cashmere knew it; she focused on the positive rather than the negative.

"Girl, you are looking good," she said, giving my ass a playful tap as we entered the lingerie store. "I wish I could have a stomach as flat as yours with an ass just as fat."

"You know you can if you stop playing games and workout with me some time," I said, giving the tiny pudge Cash had a poke. "Not that you need it considering how bomb your body is naturally. I'd trade you that little pudge if it meant I didn't have to watch what I ate all the time and could still have your ass."

Cash did a dramatic spin that ended with a little twerk. "Ain't it? But I still wanna make sure that when we're on the beaches of the Bahamas that I look every part of the bad bitch I was born to be. Vito needs to see me all over IG and remember that it's not wise to cheat on filet mignon with Hamburger Helper."

"Vito is not going anywhere," I promised her as I fingered a nice red bra made with Chantilly lace. "He'd have to be crazy to leave you. You're every man's dream."

"Lemme tell you something about these niggas," Cash said, as she grabbed a shopping bag and began blindly throwing panties inside of it. "A man could have a pocket full of diamonds and still pick up a dollar. It's plenty of beautiful women out here getting played."

"I guess you're right." I paused thoughtfully. "Cash?"

"Hmmm?"

"Let's say, hypothetically speaking, that Vito cheated on you—"

Cash stopped tossing panties and rolled up on me. "You saw Vito with another bitch?"

"Cash, I said hypothetically." When she didn't stop staring at me I slapped a hand to my forehead. "Lemme rewind: If you caught your man cheating on you, what would you do? Are you staying or leaving?"

"Staying," Cash said resolutely. I had let out an inward sigh until she finished with, "Staying along to fuck up him and that bitch. I'm setting his house on fire, reporting his ass to the cops, and I'mma make sure to put sugar in the tank of his car. In short: I love myself too fucking much to settle and deal with any bitch ass nigga who's sleeping on my worth."

I nodded along, casually playing with the bra on the mannequin. "True, true."

"Why? Is Amir cheating on you, Yara?"

"Of course not. One of my coworkers got cheated on by her boyfriend and she was asking me whether or not she should stay."

"Which coworker?" Cash asked, giving me the side eye. "Homegirl with the unibrow and lazy eye?"

"Yeah…her."

"Well maybe one day we can give her a little makeover or something. Make her feel better," Cash thought resolutely. "Anyway, why did you drag me here? You know damn well the last thing I need to do is buy any more lingerie. Me and Vito go through the same song

6

and dance: I try to show it off and he chases me around the house trying to rip it off."

"I need to find something Amir will want to rip off of me. What do you think about this?" I asked, standing next to a powder pink silk slip and matching robe.

Cash cocked her head to the side. "Nah. That has honeymoon all over it. You need something like this…"

My jaw dropped when Cash went from classy to the trashiest piece of clothing in the store. It was this fishnet situation I didn't even think would hold one of my ass cheeks. I shook my head at her, saying with my eyes, *ain't no way in hell.* Cash flicked through the rack and pulled out one my size, holding it up to me with a wide smile.

"You said you wanted something he would rip off. All that little pink outfit will do is look pretty. Right, Sharise?"

Sharise?

I turned around and there was Sharise, all smiles and giggles as she approached us. I told myself not to, but I couldn't help but check her out and wonder what she had on me. Sharise was a stunner that was constantly mistaken for Eva Marcille, with her long legs, hazel eyes, and flawless caramel skin making her a dead ringer for the model. I knew I was no model, but I was pretty. Or at least that's what Cash told me, and she was never one to lie. Sharise snapped me out of my trance with a hug and kiss on the cheek. It took everything in my existence not to wipe it off and slap it back on her face.

"Hey, boo," I said, staring between Cash and Sharise. "I wasn't expecting to see you here."

"I called Cash to see what she was doing, and she said she was meeting you here to grab some lingerie. I could use a few new pieces myself so I figured why not? It's not a problem, is it?"

"Of course not," Cash answered for me. "You know Yara doesn't like surprises."

"Yeah, I was just a little thrown," I co-signed.

Sharise gave me a squeeze and started looking at lingerie, her eyes falling on the piece in Cash's hand. "This is too cute. Is this for you?"

"I picked it out for Yara, but she ain't feeling it."

"Yes I am." Both women stared at me like I was crazy. "What?"

"You weren't feeling it five minutes ago. Now because Sharise likes it, it's cool?" Cash said with play saltiness. "You tryna say my taste is bad?"

"No, I just didn't see it that well in the light. I'll take it for tonight."

Sharise posted up against one of the tables. "What's tonight?"

"I'm doing a little something sexy for Amir. Just because. I'm always at work, so I haven't been attending to him like I should."

This bitch looked me dead in the eye and said, "I think that is sooo romantic." She smiled wistfully and added, "I might do a little something for my boo too."

"You mean the imaginary one? Because we've never met him," Cash said as she continued her journey around the store with us in tow. "I'm starting to think it's because he's somebody else's man."

"Really, Cashmere? I'm nobody's home-wrecker," Sharise

retorted, and had the nerve to sound hurt by the accurate description of the situation. "My nigga is all mine. Zeus treats me like a princess."

"Oh, we get a name now?" Cash mocked. "What does this Mr. Zeus do, other than be invisible?"

"Fucks me like no other. When he's not breaking my back he's making sure my accounts are stacked."

Cash glanced over her shoulder and asked, "So when are we meeting Zeus?"

"Maybe tomorrow night at the club. He'll be the one in the VIP section buying out the bar," Sharise said with a hint of venom. "You're not the only one that can pull a baller, Cashmere."

"I never said I was. I just noticed that you've been talking about getting your back broke on the regular, but never mentioned by who. But now we know about Mr. Zeus and we'll meet him tomorrow. I, for one, am excited to meet any man that can wrangle your messy ass in."

"As you should be." Sharise eyes lit up at the sight of a two-piece set. "Oh, my boo is going to love this…"

I watched her finger the outfit and place it against her. How many times had she showed up to my house dressed in something that provocative and fucked my boyfriend senseless? Cash stepped in front of me, her eyes filled with concern.

"Yara, you good?" She glanced back at Sharise for a second. "Did the two of you have a fight or something? Had I known, I wouldn't have invited her."

I knew if I told Cash the real reason I was out buying lingerie she would flip this entire store upside down and strangle Sharise with a G-string. If there was a Zeus and he was making my homegirl happy, then maybe she would leave my man alone.

******

I came home to an empty house. Amir left a note on the fridge telling me he had a late client over at the tattoo shop. This was the third late client he had and I was starting to wonder if more than tattooing was going on.

"I guess I'll find out tonight," I muttered as I kicked off my shoes and padded to the bedroom.

I stood in the doorway taking in the scene. The room was spotless, and had I not stood in this same spot twenty-four hours ago, I would've never suspected a thing. I picked up my comforter and gave it a sniff. The smell of Tide filled my nostrils, and it was the same with the sheets. He was a wicked nigga for fucking this bitch in my house, but he had enough manners to clean the sheets. That made it worse; it told me he cared about my feelings, to a certain extent.

Didn't he?

"You know what?" I said to myself as I popped a pan of lasagna into the oven. "Stop thinking about him with the next bitch, and think of what you bring to the table."

I did just that while taking a long shower, pampering my body from head-to-toe. I did my hair in a cute little updo, slathered my body in coconut oil body butter, and slipped into the netted outfit the way Cash and the sales associate taught me. Dinner was ready, and if I did my thang right, Amir would be having me for dessert. I was smiling to myself as I lay in bed waiting for him to come home. I was so busy picturing the scene I didn't even realize I had fallen asleep. I was woken up by the sound of the front door slamming. Amir appeared seconds later, taking me in from the doorway.

"Was tonight our anniversary or something?" he asked, eyeing me nervously as he stripped out of his clothes.

"No," I yawned, sitting up and rubbing my eyes. "I wanted to do something romantic for us. You know, spice things up. It's been a while since we made love and I was missing you…"

"Damn, baby, I appreciate the gesture, but I'm exhausted. The tat I just got finished doing took five hours. All I wanna do is take a shower, eat, and go to sleep."

I opened my robe, giving him a good look at the bodysuit from earlier. "Are you sure that's all you wanna do?"

Amir bit his lip, taking in the sight. "How about you get dinner together while I take a shower? Lemme get my strength up."

"You do that."

I was smiling from ear to ear as I heated up the lasagna and garlic bread. So what if it was going on three in the morning? My man was happy to see me, something I had been dying for since this entire situation. If I put it on him right, he wouldn't even need to see Sharise tomorrow, or ever again for that matter. I was still smiling to myself as Amir came out looking like a snack in nothing but a pair of gray sweats. His dreads were tied up in a bun on his head, revealing the tats on his neck, one of them being my name. I caught myself wondering if Sharise ever saw my name and felt the slightest bit of guilt.

"What you over there thinking about?" Amir asked as he sat down across from me. "You've been quiet ever since yesterday, now you're planning romantic dinners? What's gotten into you?"

"I was just thinking it's been a while since we've spent time together, just the two of us," I said, nibbling at my food; my nerves had butterflies fluttering through my stomach.

Amir co-signed with a nod. "Hell yeah, I been at the shop every spare moment I get, and you've been working late every night for the past few months."

"Not for long."

Amir stopped chewing for a split second. "Word?"

"Yeah, hours are being cut because we're hiring some new people, so I'll be home early starting in a couple of weeks," I lied easily, knowing damn well the hours were there for me to take if I wanted them.

"That's wassup. I've been missing you around the house," Amir replied.

"Really?"

"Yara, I love you. Why wouldn't I want you home more often? We've been working opposite shifts for the longest, and I miss you." He took a swig of wine and said, "Lemme show you how much."

"Oh really?" I said, sliding out of my seat and flouncing over to him.

Amir stood abruptly, and grabbed me with the same sense of urgency. I wrapped my legs around his waist, tonguing him down as he carried me to the bedroom.

"Show me how much you been missing me," he grunted as he plopped me down on the bed.

I tucked my hair behind my ears and got to work, pulling Amir's already swollen dick from his sweatpants and placing it in my mouth. I moaned in delight at the feeling of it pulsing in my mouth as I gently sucked. Amir's intake of breath let me know I was doing my thing just right. I wrapped my hands around the shaft and became a little more enthusiastic than usual, flicking my tongue and tickling his balls. I barely found my rhythm when Amir placed his hand on the back of my head, choking me with his ten-inch dick down my throat. I gagged on it and pushed him away, highly affronted.

Amir looked pissed, then apologetic, like he got caught slipping up. "My bad, Yara, I thought—"

"You thought what?" I spat, holding my throat.

"Nothing," Amir said with his hands up. "You just got so into it I thought you wouldn't mind me choking you a little."

"Why the fuck would I like something like that?"

This was the closest I had got to asking him about his infidelity. I sat there begging him with my eyes to just come clean, be a man about his shit, but I wasn't surprised when he lied and placated me with kisses.

"I don't know. I was tripping. You forgive me?"

I nodded. "Yeah."

"A'ight, climb to the middle of the bed and let me take care of you," Amir said huskily.

I did as I was told, smiling up at him with the incident from a few minutes ago long forgotten. Amir tickled my thighs with kisses between the fishnet until he reached the crotchless opening. I stopped him before he could even think about going down on me. I didn't get off from it and he knew that.

"I thought you wanted me to take care of you?"

I scrunched my face up. "Nah, just give me the D, and I'm good."

"If that's what you want."

Amir filled me with his length, going nice and slow just like I liked. Compared to the fervent fucking between him and Sharise, this was what real love felt like. Or what I thought it was supposed to feel like, because as Amir kissed me and stroked my hair, I felt like there was something missing.

Quade

I took a pull of my cigarette and dangled it over the trail of gasoline leading to the simp ass nigga tied to the chair at the end of it. Of course the ash from the cigarette wouldn't be able to ignite the gasoline, but his dumb ass ain't need to know that. All he needed to be aware of was that if he ain't start talking, his mother wouldn't have to worry about cremating him. Zeus eyed me nervously, but remained silent like he always did when I was extracting information. His part of the game was the business and I was the muscle.

"My patience is wearing real thin, Big Boy," I said to my victim, although he was no more than 170 soaking wet. "You know how long it's been since I killed someone?"

Big Boy shook his head, "Nah, Quade. H-H-How long?"

"Like a day, which is a personal record for me. And it's all because I been playing nice with your bitch ass. Zeus has got it in his mind that you're worth more to us alive than dead...but you know what I think? I think sometimes you gotta put a little pressure under a nigga in order for him to take you more serious."

"Quade, you think if I ain't know where them niggas was, I wouldn't tell you? I told you where the rendezvous spot was. They switched up on me at the last fucking minute. I swear on my daughter,

Quade, I would tell you where your stuff was if I knew. I got kids to live for."

"Quade, he don't know," Zeus said with a shrug. "Let him go."

I took another pull of my half-finished cigarette, mulling over where I stood. I could kill this nigga and never get back the ten kilos of coke from the re-up that went awry with my lieutenant, or I could let him go and keep an eye on his ass. He knows where his friends are and it's only a matter of time before they show up. I knew exactly what I had to do. A look of relief flashed across Big Boy's face as he saw me put out the cigarette. He was so focused on that burning ember, he didn't see me brandish my Glock and put two bullets in his chest, killing him instantly. Zeus flinched at the sound of the shots before turning to me with evident disgust. I ain't give a fuck; I was made the hitta of the team because I was the only one able to pull a trigger without guilt. Zeus might've been the oldest and wisest of the Townsend Brothers, but I was the most ruthless, and giving me the job of disposer came with a price.

"Didn't I tell you not to kill him, lil' nigga?" Zeus said with his jaw set. "Now what the fuck are we supposed to do?"

"Go to the club and see which one of these broke niggas is out there popping bottles when they were begging for work last week," I said with a shrug of my shoulders. "Face it, Zeus: he wasn't giving shit up. Whatever pact they made, they kept, and if it didn't involve our coke I might be impressed."

Zeus knew I was right, which was why instead of arguing with me, he asked the next obvious question. "Where will they be tonight?"

"With new money? Probably at that new spot, Cypher. It's supposed to be a rap battle there tonight so you already know the whole hood is showing up. I'll be there in the cut on the lookout while you get a VIP section and enjoy yourself. Someone will be spooked by you being present and I'll be sure to catch them before they leave."

"How ironic," Zeus laughed as he checked his phone. "One of these hoes I been messing with for the past couple weeks has been begging me to take her out. I guess tonight is her lucky night."

"Which one?"

"Sharise."

I grimaced. "Damn, when you said hoe, I ain't know you meant 'hoe' hoe. You better be careful with that bitch; I heard she be burning."

"I ain't hitting that until I see a STD panel. She was supposed to have gone and got one a few days ago. If she knows what it is then she will have," Zeus said, shooting off a text and placing his phone back into the pocket of his Burberry trench.

This nigga was always dressed to the nines. He the only motherfucker I know that would show up to a torture session dressed like he's getting ready to walk for Fashion Week. Anyone would feel like less than next to Zeus, who was virtually untouchable in the streets, but I had lived so much of my life in sweats and hoodies, that anything else felt foreign. It might seem strange to some, but I was born to be a hitta, and the only way I was giving that up was when I was put to rest.

******

Cypher was just as crowded as I expected it to be. The dim lighting made for the perfect cover as I sipped an Incredible Hulk. My adrenaline was pumping and the effects of the Red Bull had me more amped than I should've been. I stared across the room to where my brothers were posted up for the night, laughing at the sight. Zeus had Sharise next to him, watching her with mild interest as she took shot after shot of Patrón while bopping to the trap beat playing above; my second oldest brother, Hasani, had his girlfriend, Gia, sitting on his lap feeding him curly fries; beside him was my third brother, Savion, trying to talk to the shorty next to him while her homegirl next to her stared into space. I laughed at the sight, glad to be the lone wolf of the pack because there was nothing worse then being stuck with some boring ass bitches when I could bust a nut and get back to business.

"I need three bottles of Möet and two Ace of Spades," the bottle girl said next to me.

I watched as the bartender prepped her requests, and waited to see which direction she went in. You couldn't have told me that she wasn't making it over to my brothers, but in fact, she wasn't. I downed the rest of my drink, slid out of my chair, and followed her through the club to see where she was making such a large delivery. The strobe lights bounced off of the metallic dress she wore, causing that fat ass of hers to shine like a bright beacon leading the way. I stopped short as she arrived to her destination. I was expecting to see some young niggas living it up, but instead I was greeted by a group of men around my brothers' ages. I was getting ready to turn back around and go back to my spot when I saw Big Boy's older brother, Jerry, take a seat with them niggas.

"That's how the fuck we doing shit?" I said, watching as Jerry sparked up a blunt and placed it into rotation. "Say no more, nigga."

I took a seat on the far side of the bar, which gave me a better view of the section. Every so often, Jerry would get his ass up and greet someone, slapping hands with them. It only took once for me to know exactly what the fuck was going on.

"This nigga is selling our shit in the club," I said during my call to Zeus from the alley next to the club. I glanced back at the service door to make sure I wasn't talking too loud. "And he ain't alone; some niggas I ain't never seen before got a table full of bottles. I'm starting to feel like they're taunting me, Zeus. They know I'm here and they want me to see them spending off of our backs!"

"Quade, calm the fuck down," Zeus hissed into his phone. "Nobody is taunting you. You ain't had nothing else tonight other than a drink, have you?"

"Of course not; I told you I was leaving that shit alone and I did," I spat back, not liking the turn of the conversation. "Enough about me; you need to get Jerry somewhere that I can handle him."

"Quade, how do we even know he has our product? You're leaping before you look."

"Whether he has it or not, we got niggas in our territory making moves that we ain't approve of. That's an automatic violation and I ain't standing for that shit. If you don't find a way to get me Jerry, then I'm walking right back into that club and bussing on all them niggas."

"Quade—"

I hung up my phone, no longer in the mood to hear Zeus and his perfectly thought out scenarios. I reentered the club at the same time I saw Jerry walking with two white girls towards the bathroom. I knew that was my opportunity to get exactly what I wanted. Part of me wanted to bust in there and handle that nigga, but another part reminded me the last thing I needed was to catch the attention of some little white girls looking to score. They scurried out a few minutes later, giggling, and one of the girls mumbled, "I can't believe you just did that." I knew what it was and slipped into the bathroom as they left. Jerry was still in the bathroom laughing and fixing his pants as I blocked the bathroom door. He went from getting his shit wet to lubricating the barrel of my Glock, which had taken his brother only hours ago.

"You thought I wasn't gon' catch on to you?" I asked, shoving the gun deeper down his throat. "I know you motherfuckers set my lieutenant up to get robbed for them keys. Where the fuck they at? With your new employers out there?"

Jerry backed up, removing the barrel from his mouth and said, "Quade, I don't know what the fuck you talking about."

"You don't know nothing about my shit going missing? Because niggas been tearing the hood apart trying to find out where it went. I guess that was foolish 'cause you niggas played smarter and not harder. Went and found some niggas with pull to make something happen for you."

"Quade, I'm telling you that—"

"Big Boy told me everything," I lied, studying him, watching for the slightest change in attitude. "He told me how you all planned this shit out real smooth. That J Reed kept his shit 'cause he a cokehead. Kenny's the brains of the team so I'm sure he brokered the deal, got a larger cut, and flipped at least half of it by now. Big Boy wanted his so he could get his kids out of his baby mom's house 'cause her boyfriend be on some funny shit. You found some suppliers and made a deal. They got you here seeing whether or not you would fit in with their team."

Jerry shook his head in disbelief. "I knew he would fucking snitch. Where the fuck you got him at?"

"He should wash up in the Hudson River by the morning, maybe another day depending on the current," I said with a shrug.

"You killed my brother?" Jerry's eyes glistened. "You murdered my fucking brother?"

"Nigga, I don't know why you're crying; you're next."

Unlike his brother, Jerry decided that he wanted to go out like a real nigga. I figured the least I could do was have some fun with him before I murked his ass. He came charging at me like an angry bull, eyes teary and nose snotting. I cocked my fist back, knocking him square in the face. He snapped back quick, hitting me with a strong right hook that sent me toppling into one of the stalls. I was done playing with his motherfucker.

"Aight, bet," I said, lifting my foot and kicking him straight into the row of sinks.

Jerry hit them with a thud, toppling to the floor despite the show of strength he made seconds ago. "You a pussy ass nigga," he spat as he stood on shaky feet. "You ain't shit without a gun, are you? I've heard that every nigga you ever killed got hit with bullets, maybe a knife, but none of them have ever been done with your bare hands, have they?"

"This is what the fuck you wanna talk about with your last few minutes of life?" I asked with a chuckle. "How I kill people? Nigga, it ain't none of your fucking business how I kill people."

"Your father used to do it with his bare hands whenever he could," Jerry said, giving me the slightest amount of pause as he backed away from my gun. "I heard from my pops that Big Zeus would crack necks, choke a nigga until he stopped breathing, he used to suffocate some, beat others, but the one thing he always did was make sure he handled them with his hands. Why? Because he wanted to feel the life leave their body. But his youngest son does the opposite; you fear killing with your hands because you fear death."

"I face death all the time," I said, my gun steadily following him towards the stalls.

"Blindly. In situations where you might go fast, but you've never been in a situation where you might suffer. You're scared of losing your life as much as I am right now, which is why you won't kill me."

"And why the fuck is that?" I asked, cocking my head to the side.

"Because if you kill me, then you gotta kill her," Jerry said, charging into a bathroom stall.

I almost squeezed off two shots when I heard a girl scream.

"Fuck," I hissed, thinking I should've checked to make sure no one else was in here before I charged on his ass.

I kicked the last stall door open and there stood Jerry holding a girl. I recognized her immediately—she was one of the girls sitting in the VIP section with my brothers. Tears streamed down her face as Jerry held a gun to her head, smiling at the setting of my jaw.

22

"No one will blink twice if you kill me; I'm a street nigga just like you. But look at her? Someone this beautiful will be missed," Jerry rationalized. "You either kill the both of us, or you let the both of us go. Which one will it be?"

"I'd rather lay the bitch to rest than let you walk out of here with another day to plot my downfall," I said, much to Jerry's surprise.

His eyes widened, and he said, "What the—"

Pop!

All I needed was one second of surprise for his grip on his gun to slacken. My bullet tore through his brain, creating the worst case of blowback, sending bits of his brains splattering the bathroom wall. Jerry's gun popped off a shot inches from the girl's face as his body hit the floor. Shorty's mouth opened to let out a loud ass scream, but was silenced by my gun pressing against her chest.

"I just saved your fucking life and you're about to thank me by making shit hot?" I hissed through gritted teeth. "Make me put one in you, with your ol' ungrateful ass."

She went from scared to angry. "Ungrateful? You just killed a man right in front of me, barely missing me by inches, and I'm supposed to *thank you?* You must be out of your fucking mind."

"I must be because I'm still sitting here arguing with your dumbass instead of getting the fuck outta here," I said as I backed out of the stall. I closed the stall door as I tried to figure out what I was supposed to do with her.

I couldn't let her stay here as a potential witness to the cops, but I couldn't take her with me. I placed my gun to the stall door and took a deep breath as I readied myself to kill her. Once again, my hand was on the trigger when she gave me pause.

"Make it quick."

"What?"

"I know you're standing out there trying to decide whether or not you're going to kill me. Make it quick."

I placed my burner in my pocket and opened the stall door. "What? I wasn't going to kill you." When she didn't look convinced, I added, "I wasn't sure what my exit plan was."

She nudged her head at the window up high. "You could leave through there. The drop isn't too high."

Why didn't I see that? I said to myself. Oh yeah, because I'm still trying to figure out what the fuck to do with this girl. "You're right. I can climb out and catch you when you come out."

"What? I'm not going anywhere with you."

"I can't leave you here alive covered in blood," I rationalized. "The line behind that door is growing and it's only a matter of seconds before someone comes looking. Damn, my brother just texted me. He said women are asking questions about the bathroom. We need to get out of here."

I shrugged out of my hoodie and tossed it to shorty. She shrugged into it and stood there awkwardly. With one fluid jump, I was holding on to the window and halfway out. I held my hand out to her and after a moment's hesitation, she grabbed it and held on to the window. I jumped down and waited for her to climb over.

"Wipe your prints off of that window," I told her.

"Are you sure you're going to catch me?" she squealed.

I nodded even though she couldn't see me. "I promise, now hurry the fuck up."

"Don't curse at me."

"Then don't take forever to climb out the bathroom window. Act like your nigga on the other side of that door or something, but hurry up."

She let go, flying straight into my arms. I buckled in surprise at the weight—she was heavier than she looked—but I didn't hesitate much longer, carrying her to my car parked at the end of the alley. After securing her in the passenger seat, I slid into the driver seat, took a deep breath, and rode out. Nothing was popping in front of the club, letting me know that no one was on to us. I glanced at the time on the radio and laughed to myself. Ten minutes. All this shit popped off in ten minutes. I was still laughing to myself when a stirring beside me interrupted it.

"What are you laughing about? You just killed a man," shorty said, her tone laced with disapproval.

I shrugged. "He had it coming. If your nosy ass was listening in that stall then you know I handled him for a good reason. You never had a reason to kill someone?"

"It doesn't matter whether or not I've had a reason. You killed someone and I have to spend the rest of my life reliving it in the back of my mind."

"I can solve that problem," I said easily, cussing myself for not killing her when I had the chance. "All it takes is a bullet."

"A bullet that you don't have since I have your gun pointed at you. Yeah, you gave it to me in your hoodie," she said triumphantly.

I slowed to a stop at a red light and turned to her, smiling wide. "And become an accessory to murder? Go ahead, bitch, make my fucking day."

"Don't call me a bitch!"

"Don't do bitch shit and I won't have to call you one!" I barked back, causing her scary ass to jump. "Let me tell you something about the type of nigga I am, if you haven't noticed yet. If you ever point a gun at me, make sure you pull the fucking trigger. Don't hesitate, just pull it, because if you don't, it'll be the last decision you ever make. So I'mma be nice tonight and let that shit slide because you're on some PTSD shit, but the rising sun signals a new day. Don't get me fucked up with these other niggas; when I aim, I never miss. Now take my gun out of that hoodie and put it where I can see it."

She did as she was told, pulling the gun from her hoodie pocket and placing it into the glove compartment. Her hand dug into the hoodie again, this time emerging with my phone. "Someone's calling you."

"Answer it and place it on speaker," I commanded.

She did as she was told, and seconds later, Zeus's voice filled the car. "The mess in the women's bathroom..."

"I did what the fuck I had to do and if I didn't, we wouldn't have known what happened. The only thing I regret is not getting the names

26

of those niggas he was sitting with, but that can be handled later on."
Zeus was trying to make this my fault when it was his; if he ain't want
me to start no shit he shouldn't have agreed to my plan. "You handle
the clean up?"

"Don't I always?"

"Cool."

"Before you hang up…Sharise said her friend went to the
bathroom and hasn't come back yet. Have you seen her?"

I glanced at shorty. "What she look like?"

"Her name's Yara. She's about 5'5", brown skinned, curly hair up
in a high bun, small eyes, thick as fuck…shit, when I saw her walk in
with Sharise and their other friend, I felt like shooting myself in the
foot; I got the ugly friend," Zeus laughed. "Anyway though, have you
seen her?"

"Yeah, she sitting right here next to me on speaker."

"Deadass, nigga?" Zeus said incredulously.

"Yeah, she was in the bathroom when I had my little 'conversation'
with Jerry."

"Do we have to worry about her saying anything?"

"No," Yara cut in. "As far as I'm concerned, I got into an argument
with my boyfriend, and went home. I won't even mention this to my
girls."

"Aight," Zeus said. "Quade, take care of her."

"Bet."

The call disconnected, and we sat in a companionable silence.

I wasn't big on music, but I could tell that it might ease the mood, so I turned on the radio. Some Bryson Tiller joint was playing and Yara quickly changed the station to Pop.

"What the fuck did Bryson Tiller do to you?"

She shook her head. "You wouldn't understand."

"Try me."

"My boyfriend likes to fuck to it."

"Ain't nothing wrong with that."

"I'm not the one he's fucking."

I let out a whistle. "So then why is he still your boyfriend?"

"Because he loves me. He's the only man that has ever taken the time to know me, my wants, my dreams, my aspirations. I can't imagine not spending the rest of my life with him, and I don't plan to. All relationships go through a rough patch. That's all this is."

I scratched the back of my neck, unsure of what to say next. When it came to dealing with women, I had a few I kept in rotation because they understood that I wasn't looking for anything serious. I stopped by, got a nut, maybe a home cooked meal, and I went right back grinding. All of this staying and being a doormat shit was a foreign concept to me. Shorty was bad—she managed to catch the eye of Zeus—and if I had to guess, maybe there were some self-esteem issues going on, but the best way for her to figure that out was by her damn self.

"Well, I wish you the best of luck with that. Who knows? Maybe you staying out all night will create some dialogue between the two of you."

"Who says I'm staying out? You're taking me home."

"All this time we been driving, have I asked you where you live? I didn't, because you're coming home with me for the night."

"Excuse me? I want you to take me to my house right now!"

"Covered in another man's blood and brains? Nah. You got two options: come home with me or go home to glory. Take your pick."

"You wouldn't kill me after your brother told you to take care of me."

"He ain't say take care of you; he said take *care* of you. Meaning that if I have to handle you…"

"Fine, whatever," she said, sinking into her seat.

"You hungry?" I asked as we closed in on a Popeyes. "Ain't shit to eat at my spot."

"I don't eat fast food."

"Suit yourself," I said, pulling through the drive-thru. I shouted into the intercom, "Lemme get a twelve piece meal. Make the sides red beans and rice and mashed potatoes. Throw on a large order of fries and a gallon of sweet tea."

"All that grease? I guarantee you won't make it to forty," Yara tsked.

"I don't expect to make it to thirty, but that's a story for another day," I said, pulling up to the window.

I knew she probably thought I was crazy, but it was true; wildcards like me don't last too long. Death was a part of life and by embracing it, I felt invincible. I told her as much when we pulled off with my Popeyes

29

safely tucked away in the back seat.

"I mean that's good for you and all, but I plan on living a full and happy life. Telling my grandchildren stories, growing old with my husband, pretty much living happily ever after."

"Sounds boring as fuck," I said absentmindedly.

"Boring is relative to what goals you have for yourself."

"If you say so..."

We finally arrived at the small apartment building I lived in. Out of all my brothers, I lived way below my means. I could've easily bought a Harlem brownstone like Zeus, or a condo in Fort Greene like Hasani, or rented in East New York like Savion, but living in one of the last rough parts of Bed Stuy made me feel comfortable. Everyone minded their business on the way to and from work, which was exactly what I needed on nights like this. There wasn't a soul in sight as we hopped out of my burner car and headed into the three family building.

"I'm sure you're used to living somewhere real nice, but I'm not too into designer spots," I said as I led her to my second floor apartment. "Outside doesn't look the best, but the inside is decent."

"Damn," was all I heard her say as we entered the apartment. "You've got a lot of...space."

I had the basics in each room—a futon and television in the living room, a table in the kitchen, and a comfortable king-sized bed—but that was where my furnishings stopped. I barely spent any time here, and it was better for the place to be half lived in just in case I had to leave on a whim. I placed the bag of Popeyes on the counter, kicked off my sneakers, and started down the hall with Yara following behind me like a lost puppy.

"I need you to place everything you have on in one of the plastic bags underneath the cabinet," I said once we were in the guest bathroom. "Your bra, panties, everything. I'll give you something to put on for tonight. There's shampoo, conditioner, and everything else you might need underneath the cabinet as well. Yell if you need anything, aight?"

"Okay," she said shakily. "Thanks."

I left her alone and took care of myself, taking one of my very thorough showers, making sure I got rid of all incriminating evidence. Once I was finished, I came out to grab something to eat and found shorty nibbling on a chicken wing with a small scoop of mashed potatoes, a cup of sweet tea to her left.

"After all the drama and fear wore off, I got a little hungry," she admitted with a nonchalant shrug. "Sue me."

"Don't worry about it," I said, rummaging through the bag for a breast and my fries. "I knew you would break and eat something."

"So...where am I sleeping?"

"In the room. I'll take the couch."

Yara's eyes widened apologetically. "I don't wanna put you out. You can take the bedroom and I'll take the couch."

"You think I'm gon' let you sleep out here by yourself so you can sneak home while I'm sleeping? Nah, I'm good on that."

"You mean to tell me that after everything we've been through you're really scared of me running off and telling the cops? Wouldn't I have done that already when I was in the bathroom by myself?"

She had a valid point, but I didn't plan on giving her the benefit of the doubt. "Nope. You're taking the bedroom and if you need anything, I'll be out here."

"I don't wanna sleep by myself tonight," she admitted, hanging her head in embarrassment. "I keep replaying that scene in the bathroom, and it's just as ugly as the last time. I would rather be in my bed forgetting all of this, but that isn't an option. Do you think you can handle sharing a bed with a woman and nothing happening?"

"Of course I can," I said confidently, although the longer I took in Yara under the bright lighting of the kitchen, I became slightly unsure.

She was every part as bad as Zeus described and more. He was right about her body, but what he hadn't mentioned was that Yara could put on anything and fill it out just right. Shorty was looking extra delectable in the plain white tee she wore with a pair of my basketball shorts. Once I was done getting my fill of her body, I finally made it to her face. She had beautiful delicate features, and her doe eyes were filled with this rare innocence, making me wonder how that was still possible in this day and age. I must've made her nervous with all of my staring because she started nibbling on her juicy lower lip with a pair of perfect, white teeth.

"Okay, so I guess I'll see you in a minute," she said, hastily clearing up her mess and placing it in the trashcan.

I watched her walk away, that fat ass of hers swaying from side-to-side as she hurried down the hall. "Aight."

Zeus had left me a few choice text messages I read as I finished my food. He could be mad if he wanted to, but he wasn't going to do anything. Hasani sent me a text reminding me that we needed to meet up and try to figure out who Jerry had been hanging with at the club. Savion's thirsty ass asked me to get some information from Yara about her friend. Overall, it was stuff I could deal with in the morning.

"You still awake?" I asked as I slid into bed.

Silence.

I took that as my cue to get some rest since tomorrow was proving to be a long day already. Normally, I had trouble falling asleep, except Yara's soft snores eased me into one of the best night's sleep I had since I was a kid.

Yara

"You sure you good from here?" Quade asked as he stopped a block away from my house. "I can take you all the way in."

"No, you can't; the last thing I want is my boyfriend seeing me with you and getting the wrong idea," I said, staring down at the Adidas tracksuit I was wearing. "He's already going to be suspicious considering that I'm coming home dressed in something completely different."

"If he hasn't noticed that you know he's cheating, what makes you think he'll notice you have on different clothes?" Quade countered smartly.

I cut my eyes at him. "I didn't mention my personal problems for you to throw them up in my face. You know what? Why am I even still here talking to you? See you around."

I hopped out of Quade's car with the quickness, slamming his door extra hard and storming down the street. He followed behind me, and only sped off when I arrived at the entrance to my apartment complex. I swear he acts exactly how he looks—childish. With soft caramel skin, large doe eyes, pouty lips, and a boyish grin, the last profession you would expect Quade to work in was professional killing. He wasn't even built like a hit man. His frame was slight yet solid, which caught me off guard when I fell into his arms last night. I was in the middle of danger, yet I felt…safe. I felt safe the entire night even though everything about Quade and his outlandish behavior told me not to. I was still replaying the night in my head when I stepped into the house.

"Where the fuck have you been!" was the first thing I heard.

Amir jumped up from the couch, stepping to me as he studied me from head to foot. I was wearing a pair of classic shell toed Adidas with a matching track suit, something that was out of character for me. I had woken up to the clothes laid out and instead of being ungrateful to Quade, who went out of his way to find me something nice to wear, I put them on without pointing out how obvious the outfit was.

"Amir, it's too early in the morning to be starting a fight," I said, waving away his attitude as I made my way to the bedroom. "I've had a long night, and all I wanna do is take a long shower and climb into bed."

Amir grabbed my offending hand and bent it back, causing me to yelp in pain. "Don't walk away from me," he said through gritted teeth as he slammed me against a wall. "I have been up all night worried sick about you. Calling you, texting you, and I was close to calling the cops had you not came waltzing through the door without a care in the world. Now I won't ask you again: where the fuck have you been?"

"I spent the night with my girls," I whimpered, the pain in my arms radiating upwards. "Let go of my hand, Amir. You're hurting me."

"I called Sharise. She said you went home way before her and Cash, so don't even try to use her as an excuse. Tell me the truth, Yara." Amir pressed my wrist back. "Tell me!"

"I was by myself!" I cried, but it was too late; my wrist snapped back with a loud crunch.

I felt my body grow hot, my vision blurred, and I felt faint. Amir let go of my now limp wrist, his expression apologetic. He tried to reach out to see how bad the damage was, but I refused to let him get any closer. I ran into the bedroom and kicked the door closed behind me. My wrist was bent at an awkward angle with the pain radiating up my arm in waves.

"Baby, let me in so I can look at it!"

"No!" I screamed back, tears welling in my eyes. "Get the fuck out so I can call the ambulance!"

"Yara—"

"GET OUT AMIR!"

I cried as quietly as I could, only letting out the sob caught in my throat when I heard the front door open and close. I took a seat at the edge of the bed and called 911. The operator asked me what happened repeatedly and I lied easy enough, claiming that I tripped over the carpet in my living room and fell awkwardly. A kick and shift of the furniture was all I needed to make it believable. She might not have been here anymore, but my mother's stories were living on in me and I had no idea whether or not that was a good or bad thing. Of course there were questions at the hospital, but when Amir showed up playing the part of the concerned boyfriend, they went out of the window. I allowed him to dote on me as the nurse watched, but once she disappeared to get my discharge papers, I shrugged out of his arms.

"You still mad?" Amir asked, and had the nerve to look surprised.

"It was an accident, and had you answered me when I asked you where you were the first time, this wouldn't have happened."

"So this is my fault?" I hissed, holding up my strained wrist nestled safely in a cast. "Because I wouldn't answer a question you think it gives you the right to put your hands on me?"

"I was just trying to get your attention."

"You need to find a better way of doing it," I shot back. "I wasn't with my homegirls last night. I got upset after we argued and went to a hotel. My dress got messed up at the club so I bought another outfit to wear home. That's all."

"If that's the case then why didn't you tell Sharise you were leaving?"

"Because Sharise isn't my fucking mother," I shot back, my temper steadily rising. "Why are you all of a sudden talking to Sharise about me anyway? For someone who said she isn't my real friend, she's the first person you hit up to know my whereabouts. Why not call Cash? I was out with her too."

"I don't have Cash's phone number."

"How did you get Sharise's?"

"Listen, I ain't come here to play 21 Questions with you," Amir said warningly. "I was wrong for what happened back at the house, but I wasn't wrong for being worried about you. You're my lady; I'm supposed to be worried sick when you don't come home. If you want someone that's not gon' question you out of concern, then maybe you need to look elsewhere."

As much as I didn't want to admit it, he was right. He shouldn't be made to feel bad for caring about me. "I'm not looking anywhere else, Amir. And you can't get rid of me that easily either. But I need for you to trust that no matter where I am, I'm always being faithful to you."

"You're absolutely right," Amir said, pulling me in for a gentle kiss.

"Aww, how sweet," the doctor said with a laugh. "Here are your discharge papers. I need you to sign this copy for me, and the other copy is for you…"

I signed my discharge papers, accepted my prescription for painkillers, and we were off. Amir carried all of my possessions like a true gentleman as I fingered my brace, wondering how I would get any work done. As the manager of a gym, having such an injury was a major hindrance. Most of my day was spent typing reports, cleaning equipment, and even assisting in classes if it was slow enough.

"Joel is going to have a fit over this," I huffed. "It's bad enough he's trying not to give me my raise despite how hard I've been working, now he'll really try to play me."

"Don't worry about that cornball ass nigga. Like I already told you, it ain't nothing for you to stay home and take care of the house. I'm making more than enough to hold us down. I'm completely booked this week. A group of brothers from Miami came up here just to get tatted by ya man. I'll be working on one a day and walking away with a minimum of twenty stacks by the end of the week."

"You already know I'm not quitting my job to be a stay-at-home girlfriend. We don't have any kids so there's no excuse for me to not be out there grinding to make sure home is taken care of," I replied. "I know

I don't make as much as you, but every penny counts."

"I don't disagree with that, but my moms was a stay-at-home mom. I loved coming home and knowing she was there with a snack ready before dinner. When my pops got home, she would have a beer waiting for him. That's what I want for us, but you act like staying at home or having a baby is beneath you."

"It's not beneath me, but I need a ring and marriage license before I pop out a baby," I said unapologetically. "Amir, you know my story and why a formal commitment means so much to me."

"I do know why it means so much to you, but it goes both ways. How can I give you a ring without knowing whether or not you can hold the house down? Prove to me you're worth having a ring and maybe you'll get one."

I scoffed. "Sitting in the hospital lying about how my wrist got sprained isn't holding you down? We've been together for how many years, Amir? Show me some security and maybe I'll leave my job, but for right now, I'm not going anywhere."

I wasn't sure how we even reached this subject, but I knew I was over the arguing. The rest of the ride was spent in a stifling silence. It was crazy how calm I was hours ago having a dead man's blood all over me, but this conversation about the future had me tense. Amir's phone was the only thing to break the silence, buzzing every five minutes like there was a fire or something. He didn't check it once, so I knew it had to be Sharise hitting him up to see where I was. With the way I was feeling, I had half a mind to call her and tell her my damn self.

Amir pulled up in front of the complex. "I gotta make a quick run to the shop to set up for tomorrow. I spent so much time sitting up last night waiting on you I let my work suffer."

"What time should I look for you?" I asked like I cared.

"When I get here."

"Whatever," I huffed, hopping out the car and slamming the door extra hard. "See you when I see you."

I stormed up the pathway of the apartment complex, with the argument running through my head. There was a point during our relationship where I was considering giving up my beliefs and having a baby with Amir—my baby fever had been ignited by one of my coworkers showing off pictures of her newborn daughter. However, walking in on the so-called love of my life fucking one of my best friends changed everything. Just when I thought the problems between Amir and I were fixable, I have to find out that he wants me at home barefoot and pregnant. Was this why he was fucking Sharise, whose goals were to be a kept baller wife? I wouldn't have time to answer that question because Raz came around the corner, scaring the hell out of me.

"My bad, Yara," Raz said apologetically, but there was no sign of an apology in his eyes the way they skimmed over my figure in the fitted tracksuit. "I ain't mean to scare you."

"It's cool," I said with a wave of my hand.

I went to step around him when he stopped me. Raz had been checking me out since I moved in with Amir. I was by no means offended by being on his radar with his Lloyd looking ass, but if there was one thing I didn't do, it was mess. Shitting where I lay my head was a big no-no, although Raz was tempting. Today he was dressed in a white tee with gray sweats, and I had to admit, the temptation grew a tad bit more with every move he made in them.

"I saw you crying the other day, and I wanted to make sure you were good," he said. His eyes, roamed over my body again, except on this trip they noticed my brace. "You hurt yourself?"

"Yeah, I had a little accident. It's nothing. I'm also doing good," I said, trying to move around him, only to be stopped once again. "Raz, I don't think we should be out here talking too long. The last thing I want is for your baby mother to get the wrong idea."

"Why you gotta bring her up? We're not even together." I wasn't even surprised by his universal fuckboy reply. "We just so happen to be cohabitating in the same house."

"Just like I'm happily cohabitating with my boyfriend," I said, motioning to my apartment.

Raz shook his head. "No, you aren't. I saw the pain on your face as you ran out of here. You caught them, didn't you?" When I didn't answer, he continued, "They been meeting up for a minute now. Sometimes shorty will double back after you left just to be with him. I've wanted to say something, but this felt like one of those things you needed to find out on your own."

"Yup," was all I could muster up.

"You deserve better, Yara. I know you think just because of the situation I got going on that I can't give it to you, but I will most definitely try if you let me," Raz said, placing a comforting hand on my shoulder. "Lemme show you how a real nigga does it."

I opened my mouth to reply when I heard a familiar voice from around the corner. Raz dropped his hand as his baby mother, April, came around the corner with their daughter. Her eyes flickered between the two of us as her mouth set into a grim line. *And I thought Amir was sloppy,* I thought as I finally made my way around Raz and past his rabid baby mama. She was fiending to say something to me with her pit bull looking ass. Their daughter was gorgeous, but I knew it had nothing to do with her Grimmus looking mama.

"So warming up the car turned into you trying to get with these neighborhood hoes?" April shouted loud enough for me to hear. "That's what the fuck we're doing, Rashad?"

"Man, shut the fuck up before I don't take your ass nowhere," Raz barked back. "What I told you about trying to embarrass me out here?"

I laughed to myself as I listened to the fading sounds of the couple bickering. Niggas were always trying to be on some slick shit; this wasn't my first time running into one of these complex thots acting like they weren't in full-fledged relationships, and it wouldn't be the last. With Amir's infidelity known, I was starting to wonder if I had to worry about him having a hoe or two around here. No one ever approached me, and I never got the stink eye from any of these hoes, but if Amir could get my friends to smile in my face then I'm sure the neighbors would be nothing.

******

If walls could talk, mine would have nothing to say. Amir and I hadn't uttered a word to each other since he dropped me off home from the hospital. Normally, I wouldn't take too well to us going to bed angry, but every time I felt a pang in my wrist, I knew this wasn't my fight to end. My job felt like I should cash in some of my vacation days to heal properly, which left me sitting at home alone. Sharise came over a few times, but around three she would claim she had a lunch date with Zeus. Cash shot her a funny look, which I questioned while we were alone.

"I'm sitting here listening to her lying ass because both she and I know that she is not going to see Zeus."

"I thought that was her man?"

"Girl, after you went home there was a show. So it's me, Zeus, his thirsty ass brother, Savion, and Sharise. Sharise is all up on Zeus in the front, but I could tell that he really wasn't feeling her. She gets to whispering in his ear, rubbing on his leg, and he shuts that shit down completely. Then he asked her for some type of papers and she got to playing stupid. He wasn't feeling it and promptly dropped us off at her place. I would've known more, but Savion's annoying ass kept asking me questions and stuff like I ain't tell him I got a man."

"Sharise? Shut down? Damn, I wonder what papers he asked for."

Cash cocked her brow at me. "What papers do you think he asked her for? He wanted to know whether or not that bitch was burning, and apparently her hot in the box ass had something to hide. That's your best friend: who she fucking?"

It was no secret that Cash and Sharise had a love/hate relationship. I had met them at different times in my life, with Cash being my roommate from the group home I was raised in, and Sharise being a college friend. While they had the same taste in nearly everything, the two stayed beefing every now and again. They were both my best friends, and I brought them together as often as I could, but sometimes one rubbed the other the wrong way, which left me playing the mediator.

"Hell if I know," I said, focusing on the ratchet television show playing. "You know when it comes to boyfriends, Sharise plays her cards close."

"Well whoever it is might've gave her some shit, because that's the only reason I could see her hiding information from Zeus. I don't know why she even played herself knowing his past."

My brows furrowed. "What past?"

"You don't know about the Townsend Brothers?" Cash said, her brows disappearing beneath her Gucci headband. "Their mother died of AIDS. Her late husband's best friend gave it to her. Big Zeus trusted his family with Boyd and he did them dirty: stole their money, made their mother sick, and disappeared. No one's ever asked, but they believe the Townsend Brothers killed him. Quade, the youngest Townsend, he hasn't been the same since."

"Damn," I said, placing a hand to my chest. "I can't imagine what he must be going through."

Cash cocked her head to the side. "Who?"

"No one."

"That's not what you said. You said 'him,' like you were talking about one of the Townsend Brothers. Lemme find out you didn't bring your ass home on Saturday night and you were out with Quade's little crazy ass. Don't get me wrong; he's cute, and I'm sure he's paid, but that boy has a screw loose. I've seen him pistol whip niggas in broad daylight." Cash leaned in, studying my eyes for the slightest hint of deception. "Nah, you're a little too straight laced for Quade."

I let out a sigh of relief, but that didn't stop me from asking, "What's that supposed to mean?"

"It means that you're an amazing person, but Yara, you're nobody's wild child. You play it safe, color in the lines, and would wear a life vest before even rocking the boat," Cash explained with a flippant wave of her hand. "I get it; you went through some shit. However, I don't want you scared to live life because of your past."

"I'm not scared to live my life," I said, digging in my pocket for my buzzing cellphone. "Hello?"

"I need you to do me a favor," Amir said with no preamble. "I forgot a box of ink right next to the door. Can you bring it to the shop for me?"

As much as I wanted to tell Amir I would bring it whenever I felt like it, I wasn't going to fuck with the money that kept a roof over our head. "Fine. I'll be there in a few."

Amir hung up without so much as a "thank you." He was getting real bold with this attitude and it was only a matter of time before I got just as reckless. I lived in a silent house for the first fifteen years of my life; I wasn't getting ready to grow old in one.

"I cannot believe you have me carrying this big ass box in my brand new Dsquared heels," Cash complained as we walked down the block to Heavenly Sleeves, Amir's shop located in Williamsburg. "But not after making me drive us here."

"Cash, you know damn well you love any excuse to push your

new whip," I replied, glancing back at Cash's slick Mercedes Benz convertible. "You got me wanting one of these bad boys for myself."

"Then get you one."

"With what disposable income?"

"Um, Amir is pushing a fully loaded Charger. The least he could do is hook you up with something cute after breaking your wrist."

I shot her a look. "I told you—"

"I know what you told me and I know what the truth is. I've had arguments with Vito that went a little too far, and ended with a trip to the hospital."

"Vito hit you?"

"Hell no! He flexed and I threw a lamp at his ass. My aim is better than I thought. But that's beside the point; I don't want you feeling like you have to lie to me about anything, okay?"

I still felt a little bad for hiding my night with Quade from her, but knew it was for her safety. "Okay, girl. Damn, it's packed in there."

Amir's usually empty shop was filled to capacity today with nothing but niggas. He worked by appointment, so I found it hard to believe that him or his workers would book this many people for one day. The door was locked, which was strange as hell. Tired of carrying the semi-heavy box, Cash kicked the front door three times, catching the attention of everyone in the vicinity. One of the men standing next to the door opened it a crack, and proceeded to give us the third degree.

"The shop's closed for the day," he said, closing the door in our faces.

Cash kicked the door again. Dude opened it a smidge more, and I stuck my foot inside to keep him from closing it. In a polite voice, I replied, "I'm here to drop this ink off for my boyfriend, Amir. You know, the guy that runs this shop."

"Let me see if—"

"Bear, you serious right now? That's shorty hanging up in the studio," a new voice said.

Bear disappeared and we were greeted with a lion. The first thing I noticed was his mane of thick, curly hair framing his angular face. He appraised me with a pair of dreamy, chocolate bedroom eyes. One lick of his juicy lips revealed a set of gold teeth. This was one of those thugs your mother would warn you about. The ones that would lay down some serious pipe and leave you fighting withdrawals while they moved on to the next one. If he could openly eye fuck me knowing who my man was, then he was someone I needed to stay far away from.

"Are you gonna let us in or—damn," Cash said, as the box was accepted from her, and she got a good look at the caramel specimen in front of us. "Thank you for being a gentleman, unlike your nosy ass friend."

"You mean bodyguard," he said, opening the door wider for us. "Bear is paranoid when it comes to looking out for us. Sometimes our safety is more important than common sense."

We stepped inside of the shop, which reeked of loud, Black and Milds, and expensive cologne. Free of the box, Cash put on her best runway walk, catching the eye of every nigga we passed, who had no problem taking in her fat ass in the booty shorts she wore with a cropped sweatshirt. I followed along, self-consciously running my good hand over my hair to put it back in place, not that it bothered any of the men watching us. All they cared about was checking me out in my casual tube dress with a pair of Fenty fur slides. With my messed up wrist, pumps and sandals were my only choice. Judging by the look on Amir's face, he was happy I went with casual once we stepped into his studio.

"Look who I found on my way to grab my phone," the guy said with a laugh as he placed the box on the floor beside Amir, who was immersed in his sketchpad. "My bodyguard wasn't gon' let them in."

Amir glanced up from drawing to see me awkwardly standing there while Cash walked around the studio admiring Amir's artwork. I thought Amir was going to greet me with an attitude, but was pleasantly surprised when he came over and embraced me, planting a kiss on my lips and giving my butt a gentle squeeze.

"It's good to know that no matter what we're going through I can always count on you," he murmured into my ear. "Being at work has given me the time to think things over, and you're right. I wanna take you on a vacation next week so we can work on getting back to where we used to be, aight?"

"Okay," I smiled up at him.

He turned his attention to the guy, who was posted up against Amir's desk smirking. "Baby, I want you to meet Samiel, one of my new clients I'm tatting this week. Samiel, this is Yara, the future Mrs. Amir Singletary."

"Samiel Assan, but you can call me by my stage name: Ghetto," he said, extending his hand.

"Nice to meet you, Ghetto," I said, hiding my surprise at the warmth that exuded from his hands. "Well, I don't want to hold up your session. I'll see you later, baby."

Amir pecked me on the lips. "I'll see you later."

"Bye, Amir, bye, Ghetto," Cash sung as she led me out of the studio. We saw Bear standing at the door and she said to him, "You have a blessed day as well."

"You have no idea how good it feels to have this fight behind us," I said, once we were in the semi-privacy of Cash's convertible. "I wasn't sleeping too well because of it."

"You know, I never give Amir the credit he deserves, because that was one smart move he made back there."

"What are you talking about?"

"Wasn't it obvious? He only made up with you because he saw the way Ghetto was checking you out. Obviously, that nigga is used to getting whatever he wants, and it looks like you were on the menu."

"Girl, bye."

"All I'm saying is that Amir knows he has something good with you, and he isn't willing to let it go. That says a lot about where the two of you stand."

I hadn't thought about it like that. Over the past few days I had been so worried about Amir leaving me for Sharise that I never considered he hadn't because he was where he wanted to be. Our relationship was a work in progress, but I knew if we tried hard enough, we could get back to where we once were.

Cashmere

Pulling up to my Clinton Hill brownstone, I could already tell I was in for some bullshit. The music was blasting, all the lights were on in the house, and I could smell the pungent aroma of burnt food in the air. Vito was up to his shit, and once again, I would have to be the bad guy. I was halfway up the steps when someone called my name. Knowing it was one of my annoying ass neighbors, I studiously ignored them until they called me a little bit louder.

"Cashmere?"

"Yes?" I said politely, turning to find Mrs. Brampton, the lady that lived in the basement. "How can I help you?"

"I know your husband is in the music business, but I was wondering if it was possible for him and his 'posse' to practice their jam session at a more reasonable time?" Mrs. Brampton replied kindly, her small blue eyes lit up with hope.

She was a nice old white lady that always stood up for Vito and I whenever the rest of the building complained to our landlord about the noise and shenanigans that occurred in our home. I promised her that I would relay the message to Vito and made my way upstairs to our first floor apartment.

"Vito," I called out over the deafening rap music that blasted through the house. I stomped over to the Bose surround sound speakers and cut it off. "Vito!"

Silence.

I walked deeper into the house, looking for some signs of life. I found them on the bed in the form of cocaine. A whole lot of it. There was no way in hell that Vito's supplier would front him this much product, so I wanted to know where the fuck he got it from, and if I needed to pack my stuff up and lay low. As much as I loved my boyfriend of three years, I loved myself more, and if I had to walk away and leave him to clean up the mess he made again, then so be it.

"Vito!" I screamed, banging on the door. "Vito! Open up the damn door!"

I could hear the shower water running, and felt this situation going from bad to worse. I dropped my purse, shrugged out of my jacket, and used my combat style heels to kick the door in. I entered and what I found was worse than I could imagine.

"No," I moaned, holding my hands to my face at the sight of a woman lying in our shower, slightly blue. The tattoo on her left breast was familiar, and upon closer inspection, I knew exactly who this was. "Is this nigga serious?"

I turned around to look for Vito and came face-to-face with him. He looked like something out of a horror movie, with his eyes wide as he nervously looked over my shoulder at the body lying in the shower.

"How the fuck did our neighbor end up dead in our shower, Vito?" I said through gritted teeth.

"How you know she's dead?" Vito countered. "She only been in there a few minutes. I haven't been gone that long."

51

I placed my hands to my ears and shook my head back and forth, trying to block out his stupidity before I flipped out and either said or did something stupid, like end up in a house with two dead bodies. Vito brushed past me smelling like vomit, weed, and liquor.

"Sarah," Vito said as he cut off the shower. He slapped her on the face a few times. "Sarah, wake up. Sarah!"

"Vito, stop fucking screaming before someone hears you," I hissed, removing my hands from my ears. "These people listen to everything we do. The last thing we need is for them to hear you screaming the name of that man's wife, who is supposed to be home by now."

Vito slapped her again, and this time, to my immense relief, Sarah started groaning. She slowly sat up in the shower, looking around as if trying to figure out where she was. I grabbed a towel hanging on the back of the door and tossed it to Vito, who helped her to her feet. *This can't be happening,* I thought as I entered the bedroom and began cleaning up the kilo of coke sitting on my bed. Vito came out of the bathroom with Sarah, who was now dressed in her business suit. Her hair was still wet, and her makeup smudged, but that was none of my business right now. She needed to take her high ass out of this house while she was still breathing.

"You sure you don't need to go to the hospital or anything?" Vito asked her as he placed her on the bed. "You were knocked out cold."

Sarah vehemently shook her head. "Of course not; could you imagine how it would look if one of the top prosecutors for the Brooklyn DA's office showed up at the hospital coming down from a high? I'll be fine."

"So, Brooklyn DA," I said with my arms crossed, "we don't have to worry about this coming back to us, do we?"

"You think I would tell on the two of you and mess up my connection inside of the building? Now I don't have to worry about getting it through my buddy; the quality of his product is poor and ridiculously overpriced." Sarah nudged her head at the bag the coke was in. "You mind hooking me up with an eighth before I leave?"

For someone that was stupid high, Vito sure knew how to bag the coke without spilling a single drop. Sarah paid, promised to set him up with some more "clients," and was gone without a backwards glance like she wasn't sprawled out in my shower ten minutes ago. I waited for the sound of the front door closing to speak on what I just witnessed in my very own home.

"We moved out of the hood to avoid shit like this, and you bring it right into our home? Vito, you're high and drunk. Where were you? What if I hadn't of came home and found her? Do you know how much jail time we would've been facing?"

Vito ignored my questions as he carefully bagged the coke. "I met shorty at the mailbox and she happened to see a baggie in my hand when I pulled out my keys to check the mail. I invited her in to get a little sample, got a call from my boy saying someone needed some work, and handled it. The nigga was tryna haggle me, which took me away from home longer than I anticipated."

"Vito, I'm upset with finding that woman in our bathroom, and I'm really pissed with you bringing this shit into our home, but you know what pisses me off the most? You promised me you would stop sniffing your supply and you haven't."

"All I did was take a little toke to put Sarah at ease. Stop acting like I don't know how to handle myself!" Vito shot back. "I don't ever hear you complaining when you're out spending my money on clothes, your mouth was shut when I bought you that brand new whip you're pushing, and I ain't hear a mufucking word come out of your mouth when I moved you out the hood to this bougie ass neighborhood. So please stop telling me about what I need to do when I've proven that I got this."

Grabbing my purse and jacket off the floor, I made a beeline for the front door. "Have it by yourself. I'll be back when I'm in a less disgusted mood."

I wasn't the least bit surprised that Vito didn't stop me; he was probably hoping I was leaving so he could keep on getting high. This was how most of our arguments ended, with me running off to pour my troubles while Vito stayed behind and smoked his. It was getting tiring, this fighting with him, but with Vito refusing to quit getting high, we would always remain at a standstill. I couldn't go to Yara's place because she would ask me why I came back, and I already knew Sharise was probably entertaining one of the many niggas on her roster, so I opted with hitting up one of my local haunts, The Passion Palace, this small hole in the wall strip club that made the best cosmopolitans.

"Hey, Cash," Trixie, the bartender said as she placed a Cosmo in front of me. "I haven't seen you since last week. I thought things were going well on the home front."

"They were, but you already know these hardheaded niggas can't seem to get shit right," I said, downing half of my drink in three gulps. "Just when I think Vito and I are back on the right track, he has to do something stupid."

"Ain't that how it works? I stopped fucking with my man because he had it in his head that since he was bringing home the money I was indebted to him. I was an independent woman before I met you, and I'll be one after you."

"Lucky you," I said, playing with my drink. "I've never been independent. I've always had a man taking care of me, the first one being my foster mother's boyfriend. He was a fine older dude, too. At first I thought he was tryna take the pussy like a lot of those nasty mofos in the system would, but he was paying to play. He was hitting me off with money whenever I wanted, buying me the latest sneakers, getting my hair done, all for a little bit of pussy every now and again. His wife found out and had me shipped to a group home. That didn't stop me; I made sure to use my body to snag the best hustlers Brooklyn has to offer. I haven't been without one since."

Trixie shook her head. "That's swell and all, but you need to remember something: what goes up must come down. These niggas are fucking with you heavy right now, but what are you going to do when the next generation comes along and takes your crown. How old are you?"

"Twenty-four."

"You've got at least another six years left before you ain't nothing but the old bitch at the club. By then you need to secure yourself something a little more concrete. A salon, nail shop, shit, even one of these little Instagram boutiques or something. The point is: step your game up and secure your bag before you end up on a pole like the rest of these girls."

I finished off my drink, mulling over her words. She was right; I did need a side hustle of my own just in case my situation with Vito went from bad to worse, but what could a high school dropout like me possibly get into? I was still thinking of my options when Trixie placed a glass of champagne next to my fresh Cosmo.

"Trixie, I didn't order this," I said, but that didn't stop me from taking a sip. "Mmm…this is Dom P. Whoever this was supposed to be for is about to be mad."

Trixie shook her head, laughing as I gulped down the glass of champagne. "I didn't give it to you by mistake. That was from the gentleman over there."

I turned to see who my sponsor was for the night, and you could imagine the disappointment on my face when I saw who it was. *Of all the places in the world for him to hang for tonight, he had to choose here?* I thought to myself as Savion lifted his own glass of champagne and took it to the head. I mouthed a quick "thank you" and returned to my drink. Trixie, who watched the entire exchange, asked what the problem was.

"I thought you liked ballers?"

"I do like ballers, but what I won't do is get tied up with a messy one, and that's exactly what Savion Townsend is: mess."

Trixie didn't look too sure. "I won't call him perfect, but you could definitely do worse than Savion. It actually seems like you already are.

You better be nice to your next sugar daddy because this one isn't sweet to everyone."

"If you say so," I said, playing with my glass. Trixie filled it right back up. "Is he paying for this?"

"You're on his tab for tonight," Trixie replied, setting the bottle of champagne in a bucket and placing it next to me.

I smacked my lips. "In that case, lemme get an order of chicken fingers with fries and two honey mustard dipping cups."

"At least go and say thank you, with your greedy ass..." Trixie said as she headed to the other side of the bar to place my order.

I guess, I thought as I downed my flute of champagne and poured myself another one. The room tilted to the side as I stood up. I smoothed the front of my shirt, grabbed my purse, and sashayed over to where Savion was chilling. He had two strippers performing an extremely erotic table dance for him as he puffed on a blunt. They could've been fucking on the pole for all he cared, because once I started walking towards him, Savion only had eyes for me. He dismissed the girls with a lazy flick of his wrist, making it rain down on them. I took a seat next to him and watched the girls snatch up their money and run.

"I thought I was gon' have to come over there and beg for a 'thank you," Savion said through a plume of weed smoke. "Since you wanna have me begging for everything else."

I rolled my eyes so hard I saw the nigga please etched into my brain. "I don't know what kind of hoes you're used to, but that kind of shameless flirting is nowhere near as flattering as you think. I thought I could come over here and have a dignified conversation with you, but

I guess not…"

"Wait, wait, wait," Savion said, placing an authoritative hand on my thigh. "I ain't mean no disrespect, ma. That's just how I speak. Can we start over?"

"Fine," I relented, shifting back in my seat. "Thank you for the champagne. It was delicious."

"I can tell by the way you was tossing it back," Savion noted, taking another pull with those delectable looking lips of his. "You don't look like yourself, you good?"

I shrugged. "I'm good."

"Don't say you're good if you ain't good; can't nobody help you if you don't open up about what you're going through," Savion said, his once playful demeanor turning serious. "What's going on?"

"I'm starting to feel like being a kept woman isn't the right move for me. Everyone's got a hustle, and if shit goes sour with me and my man, I don't have anything to fall back on."

Savion nodded his head slowly. "Damn, I thought you was gon' tell a nigga you had an itch that needed scratching." He spotted the unamused look on my face and gave me a gentle squeeze on the leg. "I'm just tryna lighten the mood. What are you good at?"

"Nothing."

"You don't have any skills like doing hair, nails, anything like that?"

I shook my head. "I've never had to do my hair or nails. Everything's always been taken care of for me." I picked up a glass from the table and poured myself a drink. "I have no viable skills. I don't even know why I'm sitting here plaguing you with my problems."

"You're not plaguing me. I wouldn't have asked if I didn't care," Savion said consolingly. "Before you start counting yourself out, take some time to really think about what you bring to the table. I bet there's something you're overlooking and you ain't even realize it."

"Maybe…" My eyes lit up at the waitress bringing over my food. This spot made the best tenders, and after the long day I had, I was getting ready to smash all of them. Or at least I thought I was until I saw Savion eyeing them. "You want some? I mean you are paying for this, after all."

Savion accepted a chicken finger, which instantly activated his munchies. I chuckled at the sound effects he made as he chewed the chicken finger. When you were high, everything tasted extra good. I wasn't the least bit surprised when he called the waitress back for some more food.

"Can you bring two more orders of these," Savion said, motioning to the spread. "And a bottle of Henny."

"I hope one of those orders are for me, greedy," I said, motioning from my half-eaten food to the fries Savion was stuffing into his mouth. "What are you puffing on that got you this hungry?"

Savion sparked back up the once dying blunt and passed it to me. I pulled too much at once, instantly regretting it when my lungs overflowed with smoke. Tears sprang to my eyes as I daintily coughed to the side. Once I finished with my coughing fit, I turned back to see my food finished as a still laughing Savion eyed me.

"Shit is fire, right?"

I took another pull, this time slower, and said, "Where you get this from?"

"One badman from Jamaica. I gotta re-up this weekend. You should come. Who knows? While you're there you might get some inspiration."

A trip to Jamaica would do me some good, especially with everything going on in my life. I didn't wanna appear too thirsty, so I decided to play coy.

"I can't give you a definite answer yet because my girl has been in need of some extra attention since she messed up her wrist."

"Bring her," Savion said resolutely. "You can bring your other friend too if you want. I'ont know how Zeus is gon' feel about it, but he'll be aight."

"Like I said, I'm flattered, but I'll have to give you an answer tomorrow." I held out my phone. "Here. Put your number in my phone so I can call you with my decision."

"If you wanted my number, all you had to do was ask," Savion said, accepting my phone and saving himself as "Savage." I shot him a nigga really look. "I mean, I am. You can find out tonight if you want…"

"Savion…"

"A'ight, a'ight," he said, holding his hands up in submission. "I'll save it for the trip 'cause I know your fine ass is coming."

I pulled off the blunt and passed it to him. "If you say so…"

For someone that was such a brazen flirt, Savion was a halfway

60

decent conversationalist. I got to know more about him, like his upbringing with all of his brothers, and how he was the supplier for his team. However, what surprised me the most was how for every question I asked about him, he asked two about me. It had been a long time since I sat and enjoyed the company of a man that wanted to know my likes, dislikes, hobbies, and genuinely cared about the answer. I had been wined and dined at the finest of restaurants, shopped at the finest boutiques, and enjoyed my fair share of exotic vacations, but it was sitting here eating chicken fingers with Savion that I felt a real connection. Not that I would tell him though. I was still smiling over our conversation as I entered my apartment.

"Why am I not surprised," I muttered as I hit the lights, revealing my messy living room.

The worst thing that could ever happen to Vito while he was high was that he lost his car keys or something. He'd flip over couch cushions, knock over the coffee table, empty out any jacket in the vicinity, all for him to find them sitting on the kitchen counter. Like right now.

"Really?" I muttered incredulously as I walked through the equally disgusting kitchen.

A few burnt pots sat on the stove, filled with charred ramen noodles. Vito's delusional ass must've gave up because on the counter next to his keys sat a small box of pizza with two slices still left inside of it. I tossed them into the fridge along with a half-finished bottle of Pepsi. The part of me that was raised to never leave your house dirty wanted to stay up and clean this mess, but the other part, the part that was tired of cleaning up all of Vito's messes, just wanted to go to bed and leave it for tomorrow.

"Fuck this shit," I said after a few minutes of thought.

I continued to the bedroom where I found Vito sprawled out in bed. He was still fully dressed, with his dirty Constructs messing up my expensive duvet. I pulled off his shoes, stripped out of my clothes, and slipped into bed. I tossed and turned for what felt like forever as Vito slept comfortably beside me. After another hour of the same song and dance, I gave up on sleep and shot Yara a text:

Bitch, we're going to Jamaica!!!!

Yara

"Cash, how did you get tickets to Jamaica?" I asked as I flipped through my third outdated Vogue magazine of the hour. "Your birthday isn't coming up any time soon, so I know it's not a present from Vito..."

"I got connections and that's all you need to know," Cash said excitedly. "Now hurry up and get dressed so we can go to the mall and do some shopping."

"As much as I would love to, I can't. I'm at the gyno," I replied, stopping on an article featuring Rihanna. "I've been here all morning. This is exactly why I hate doing walk-ins."

"What's wrong?"

I sighed. "A yeast infection. It came on strong last night and I need it gone pronto."

"Ooo, well make sure you get your little breadbox fixed before we board this flight," Cash joked. "We can't have you out there making bun and cheese."

"Cash," I hissed as I fell into a fit of giggles, "please do me a favor and shut up."

"I'm just saying...Girl, lemme call you back. The cleaning lady is here and I need to make sure she gets every nook and cranny. Talk to you later."

"Later, boo."

I was halfway through the interview when my name was finally called. There was a little extra switch in my step, not because I thought I was the shit, but because I was itching like crazy. This was the worst infection I had yet, and I told the doctor as much.

"I tried a Monistat at home, but it just wasn't cutting it," I said to Doctor Simone as she examined me. I watched as she gathered a sample and made her way over to the microscope sitting on the counter. "Do you think this'll clear up by the weekend because my homegirl got us tickets to Jamaica. She won't tell me how, but I'm not turning down a free trip to paradise."

"Of course I can get this cleared up," she said, peeking through the lens of the microscope. "Because you don't have a yeast infection; honey, you have Trich."

"What? What is Trich?" I was panicking. "Dr. Simone, please don't tell me that's what I think it is."

"Trich is short for Trichomoniasis. It's a parasitic STD that causes odors, discharge, itching and burning, soreness…" She moved to her computer, where she began steadily typing. "When was the last time you had unprotected sex?"

"Last week with my boyfriend."

"Ahhhh…when it comes to Trich, men are typically asymptomatic. He'll need to be treated as well…"

I dressed with shaky hands, tears pooling in my eyes until they'd had their fill and slid down my cheeks. *How could I have been so stupid?* I asked myself as I wiped the tears from my face. He's been fucking my friend for God only knows how long, and my dumbass goes behind her and fucks him too? These nasty bastards burned me and it's my own fucking fault.

"Cheer up," Dr. Simone said, giving my shoulder a gentle squeeze. "This is one of the most common STDs in the country. It's completely curable, and you caught it early, which drastically decreases the chances of any long-term effects. It's not the end of the world and there isn't anything wrong with you. After taking your medication, you'll be good to go."

"Thanks, Dr. Simone," I said as I tried to keep my head from hanging. "I'll see you in a couple weeks for my follow up."

My feet barely touched the pavement outside before I called Amir's phone. It went straight to voicemail. My next call was Sharise, and I wasn't the least bit surprised to find that her phone went straight to voicemail as well. These dirty bitches were fucking each other right now, spreading their STD back and forth. The thought had me seething as I called Cash to meet me at my apartment ASAP. I spent the entire drive home with my foot shaking in anticipation of stomping a bitch out. This was it.

I had finally reached my breaking point.

******

"Yara, what's going on?" Cash asked as she leaned off of her car. "You look ready to beat somebody's ass."

"You still got your baseball bat in the trunk?"

Cash didn't hesitate to pop her trunk. She emerged with her signature metal baseball bat. She swung it once, the sound of it cutting the air pure music to my ears. "Who we fucking up?"

"You'll see in a minute," I replied, beckoning her to follow me into the complex.

Cash kept up surprisingly well for someone wearing six-inch biker boots. Her hair was in a set of cute feed-in braids, and her usually long nails were short. I knew I could count on Cash to show up ready to throw down in her usual glamour girl style.

"I take it that your trip to the doctor's office didn't go too well," she said, trying to keep the tone light as we cut through the complex. "What he gave you, bitch?"

"Trich, and the treat is a three day regimen of metronidazole."

"Oh we tearing his ass up," Cash exclaimed as we stomped upstairs to my apartment. "Lemme kick the door in."

I placed a finger to my lips, shaking my head from side-to-side. "Nah, we're gonna sneak attack their asses."

"'Their?' There's a bitch in there with him right now?" I nodded. "Open up the motherfucking door, Yara. We fucking shit up."

I unlocked the door, and opened it like a ninja. Tory Lanez "Say It" bumped through the house as usual. If I wasn't so pissed, the *is this what we're doing* look on Cash's face would've had me weak. We crept into the house like panthers, with Cash raising her bat, ready to pounce as I braced myself for what was behind this door. I opened it slowly and nearly fainted at the sight.

In the middle of my bed, riding my boyfriend, was my neighbor, Anika.

"You phony ass bitch!" I roared, charging towards the bed. "Fucking my man in my bed?"

I leapt onto the ottoman in front of my bed, using it to propel me into Anika. I crashed into her, wrapping my left arm around her neck while using my good hand to clock her upside the head. Amir jumped back in surprise for a split second, only jumping into action when he saw I had the bitch good. He grabbed me off of her, which gave Cash the opening she needed to rain down blows with her bat. There was a resounding crunch at the sound of Anika's hand being broken as she tried to deflect the blows. Cash dropped her bat and grabbed shorty by the hair, dragging her from the bed with no remorse.

"Handle your man and I'll handle this bitch," Cash said, stopping every now and again to kick a crying Anika.

I shrugged out of Amir's arms, sick to my stomach from smelling the sex oozing from his pores. It disgusted me, especially since I could see his bare dick between his legs. The sight was enough for me to turn around and slap the shit out of him. He instinctively pulled his hand back and I dared him to do something.

"Go ahead," I screamed as I stumbled from the bed. "Go ahead and put your fucking hands on me after giving me an STD and having me catch you in the bed with our neighbor. Silly me, thinking I was coming here to catch you with my best friend that you've been fucking for God knows how long."

"You know about Sharise?" Amir leaned back into the headboard in shock. "You were here the other day. I heard the door close."

"I've been here every other day listening to you fuck her brains

67

out while you think I'm working. Then you got the nerve to tell me she ain't my friend when you aren't a shining example of a human being either!"

"And she still isn't your fucking friend!" Amir countered, sliding out of bed. "Who do you think came on to me in the first place? I told you to stop leaving her here while you went to work, but you didn't listen. I woke up one morning to her sucking my dick and I didn't stop her. You wanna know why?"

"Because you're a sick piece of shit!"

"No, because she does it how I like it instead of your scared ass!" My jaw dropped in shock at his blatant accusation. "Yeah, I like it nice and nasty, Yara, something you can't do. Like get on top and ride my dick. Sharise doesn't complain when I pull her hair or smack her ass. I can get Anika to do whatever the fuck I want, unlike your spoiled ass. What did you expect me to do when all you wanna do is lie on your back and be fucked?"

"Be honest with me," I cried. "If you weren't happy then why didn't you tell me?"

"I shouldn't have to tell you how to satisfy me. I shouldn't have to apologize for every little thing I do in the bedroom either. I'm tired of it. I didn't go out looking for women to fuck; they could see how unsatisfied I was and chose to do something about it."

"I don't care if I didn't fuck you at all! That doesn't give you the right to cheat on me! It may not seem like much, but the love I have for you is greater than any amount of pussy will ever be. And it hurts me to know I mean so little to you that you'd just fuck me over for instant gratification."

Amir scratched the back of his neck. "What you tryna say? You're leaving? 'Cause there isn't another nigga out there willing to put up with what I did, dealing with your high maintenance ass."

"You know what? There might not be another man out here willing to deal with me and my issues, but I'd rather be by my damn self than lying in a mattress soaked with another woman's coochie juices next to a man that doesn't love me enough to not cheat, or respect me enough to not do it where I lay my head."

"It's like that?" Amir said, looming over me as if his intimidation would be enough to make me back down. "You're going to give up on everything we've been through over a couple bitches?"

"Are you going to stop cheating on me?" Silence. "That's what I thought. I'll pack a bag for tonight, and be back for the rest of my stuff next week when I get back from vacation."

Amir frowned his face up at the word. "Vacation?"

"Yes, a well-deserved vacation. I'mma get my mind right, work on me, and come home to live my life without you," I said, taking one last look at the former love of my life. I reached into my pocket and pulled out the paper Dr. Simone gave me. "Here's the paper you need to get your medicine for Trich. You should let Anika know her pussy is on fire. No need to call Sharise; I'll be sure to let her know."

The anger I once carried left my body, replacing it with hurt. Hurt that instead of admitting he was wrong for cheating on me, Amir made it all my fault. I was no angel, but I damn sure wasn't a devil deserving of being burned. As I stood in my closet, I decided I didn't want any of the stuff he had bought me. I'll get my own when the time was right.

"Where's your stuff?" Cash asked, her brows furrowed at the solitary Victoria's Secret Pink duffel bag in my hand.

I shrugged my shoulders. "I don't want it. He can keep it all. I'm ready to start over and I can't do that walking around in stuff the last nigga bought for me."

"Yes the fuck you can," Cash exclaimed. "You can sell it to pay some bills, give it away to the less fortunate, you can even take some of his shit with you and sell it. I'm going back inside of that house to take—"

"Cash, my dignity is more important than everything in that house. I'll be okay," I promised her. "That is, if you let me stay on your couch until I get on my feet."

"Of course, you know I'd never leave you out in the cold." Cash gave a dramatic swing of her bat. "So, where are we headed now? I hope to get something to eat; I'm starving."

"How about we go somewhere with some strong drinks? I can certainly use one."

Cash nudged me. "We can go to Sharise's Applebee's. It's close by, ain't it?"

"Yup," I said, smiling at my next stop for the day. "It most certainly is."

******

Cash was in full bird mode as she told me how she handled Anika's ass. Her hands were flopping around with each embellished word. Everyone in the vicinity was enjoying the show almost as much as I was.

"So I'm stomping her all while asking 'you like fucking in people's beds, huh?' and the bitch is just crying while begging me to let go of her. One of your neighbors came out and I thought she was getting ready to record, but she started cheering me on because Anika was tryna fuck her man too. So I'm beating her ass and—Hey Sharise!"

Everyone turned to a surprised Sharise, who gave us a little awkward wave and went back to taking orders at her table. I noticed her switch from one foot to the other, then back again. Cash took in the sight as well, her eyes flicking between the two of us. Once they lit up in recognition, I knew that was it.

Cash leaned back in her seat, sipping her margarita like she was plotting. "So, are we going to eat and then embarrass her, or embarrass her then order some food on the takeout side?"

"Now, girl," I said, cocking my head to the side. "Red Lobster is right on the other side of the mall. We ain't gotta eat shit in here."

"True, true." Cash waved her hand at Sharise before she could disappear. "Sharise! Yoo-hoo! Boo, come over here for a minute."

Sharise twitched her ass over here, her smile tight as she approached the table. "Hey ladies, what's up?"

"Nothing, we just wanted to say 'hi' and see what you've been up to," Cash said over the rim of her glass. "What time do you get off? Maybe you can stay around and have some drinks with us."

"No...I'm not really in a drinking mood," Sharise dismissed with a wave of her hand.

"Why not?" I piped up. "Because it'll have a bad reaction with the metronidazole you're taking?"

Sharise paled. "Yara, I can explain."

"Explain what? How you were fucking my man in my house while I was at work?" I screamed, catching the attention of everyone in the restaurant. "That your nasty, hoe ass was fucking my man raw and gave him an STD!"

"He gave it to me!" Sharise barked and caught herself immediately. In a calmer voice she said, "Can we please talk about this later, or when I'm not at work?"

"You think I give a fuck about your job?" I exclaimed, slapping her notebook out of her hand. "You didn't give a fuck about me or my home when you walked into it fucking my man, so what makes you think I give a half or a whole of a fuck about your damn job?"

I could see security cutting through the tables, getting ready to throw us out. I picked up my glass of water and threw it in Sharise's face. She snapped like I knew she would, pouncing on me like a wild animal. I let her get one good lick in, then hemmed her up and laid into her. Yeah, I might've gone to college and played it prim most of the time, but when I got mad, the hood in me came out. Cash jumped between the security guards, fighting them while I fought Sharise, who was good for hair pulling and scratching. I had a scratch for that ass.

"Ouch," she shrieked, trying to get away from me when I poked her ass with one of those dull ass butter knives they left at the table. "Bitch, did you just try to stab me?"

"You like being poked so damn much," I hissed, poking her ass in her arm again.

We were yanked apart by security, who escorted Cash and I out of the restaurant. I was covered in margarita, my hair was all over my head, and Cash's dress was torn. We scurried into the car and pulled off before they could call the cops on us. It was silent on the ride to Cash's apartment, with her humming "Girl Fight" under her breath. I laughed at her choice of song and next thing I knew, we were laughing together.

"Did we really just have two fights in two hours?" Cash asked, doubling over at a red light. "We haven't scrapped this much since that time we got caught stealing at Target and jumped the LP guard in the elevator. His boy came tryna back him up and he got them hands too."

I howled. "Hell yeah. Had we not been in high school they probably would've tried to press charges on us. Ugh, I needed that laugh." I paused thoughtfully. "You think Sharise is gonna rat us out?"

"If she's smart she will play deaf, dumb, and blind," Cash replied. In a serious tone, she added, "Don't let any of this get you down, girl. Sharise is a gutter rat, Anika ain't nothing but an old hoe, and Amir is trash for putting you through all of this in the course of one day. P.S.: catching that shit from Amir doesn't make you any less of a woman, you understand me?"

"I didn't even say anything that would have you thinking that I—"

"Yara, you've been hard on yourself since we were kids. I know you well enough to know you're probably cursing yourself out over someone else's shortcomings. Don't. Let's just focus on getting you good for Jamaica, where I'm sure you'll get your groove back. You hear me?"

"I hear you," I said, leaning on her shoulder. "Now let's go get something to eat. I'm starving and I wanna smell your drinks since I can't have one of my own."

"You got it, best friend, you got it."

Quade

Corrine spun around in the slinky Versace dress a few times, allowing me to appreciate it from every angle. She shot me a thousand watt smile over her shoulder. I gave her the "so-so" hand because while the dress was nice—it hugged her trim waist and fat ass like a second skin—it didn't do her justice. Corrine stuck her middle finger up and her tongue out playfully. We had been shopping for this trip for the past two hours, so I knew she had to be tired. I was too, but I wanted to make sure everything was perfect for this trip to Jamaica. This was my best friend's first trip out of the country and I wanted to make sure she was looking right.

"Quade, I don't need any of this fancy stuff. I can take my ass right to Century 21 and get a few designer pieces off season for the price of this one dress," Corrine said as she padded into the changing room. "How about we focus on finding you something to wear? Because I'll be damned if I see you chilling on a beach in Jamaica wearing that hoodie and some sweats."

"What's wrong with that?" I asked; that was exactly what I planned on wearing in Jamaica. "You already know I don't do none of this designer shit."

"I don't know why not. You know if you put some effort into getting dressed, shaping your beard, getting a fresh cut, and using lotion you might be able to find someone half decent."

I rolled my eyes at the absurdity of her statement. "Who says I'm looking?"

Corrine stepped out in a mauve romper. It was low cut in the front, which wasn't a problem being that she was an A cup on her best day, and it complimented her dark chocolate skin perfectly. She struck three poses in front of the mirror, the same silky material swishing with each movement. I gave her the thumbs up, my first one since we entered the store.

"It's about time," Corrine sung as she danced back into the changing room. "Now let's start looking around for you."

"All you got so far is that romper, some sandals, and a suitcase. We need to at least get you a couple more dresses and shorts before wrapping up."

Corrine emerged from the changing room dressed back in her street clothes, the boyfriend jeans and oversized tee the polar opposite of the Italian piece she changed out of. "How about this? We go over to Barney's and finish up there. I'll pick out some stuff in the women's section while you find some shorts and show off those little bird legs of yours. But first you need to show off that lil' chest with this."

Corrine stopped at a rack of men's silk Versace shirts. She flipped through until she found a black and gold one with dark red accents. I couldn't even lie; it was a nice ass shirt, but not nice enough for me to wear anywhere. I was poised to tell Corrine as much when she hit me with those puppy dog eyes of hers.

"Fine, I'll wear the stupid ass shirt," I muttered as she placed the clothes on the counter."

The saleswoman didn't blink twice as she read out the total. "That's will be $3,428."

"Quade, have you lost your damn mind?" Corrine mouthed as I handed the saleswoman my platinum Amex. "You know what the fuck we can do with four grand? Better yet, you know what I can do?"

I accepted the bag and my card from the woman. "You can look good on my dime."

"And pay for a semester of school," Corrine added as we left the store. "I mean I've always known you had it like that, but I ain't know you had it like that."

Being the youngest and most reserved of my brothers came with a lot of perks. Zeus paid the rent for my apartment, claiming it as an office space on his taxes, while Savion treated me to the best restaurants that money could buy in the hopes that my taste would improve. However, it was Hasani that helped my money grow by taking it and investing it in small businesses all over the city. I've had an unlimited cash flow ever since I was younger, and didn't start cashing out on it until now.

"You know I always got you, Corrine," I said, smiling down at her. "Don't ever be afraid of asking me if you need anything."

Something shined in Corrine's eyes. "I won't," she smiled. "You mind if we stop in there for a minute?"

I followed her hand to the Victoria's Secret across the street. "Aight, lets go."

With a devilish grin, Corrine tugged me across the street and into the huge lingerie store.

At once, I was greeted with the overwhelming scent of perfume sticking to my nostrils. After I got over the shock of the smell, I had time to take in the scenery. The first thought that popped into my head was that I should've waited outside while Corrine looked around. I didn't want her getting the wrong idea, especially with every piece on each mannequin screaming, "fuck me."

"I'mma find somewhere to sit while you look around," I said, motioning to a set of chairs I spotted in the cut. "This might take a while."

Corrine grabbed me by both of the hands and led me deeper into the store. "But how can you help me pick stuff out if you're sitting down?"

I opened my mouth to reply when I heard a familiar voice say, "Quade?"

Right behind Corrine was one of my hoes, Niasia, with one of her friends. I already knew they would be on some shit just by the way her and her friend were looking at us. Instead of letting go of my hands, Corrine held on to them tighter as she looked both women dead in the face. At what they took as a sign of blatant disrespect, both women headed in our direction.

"Quade, baby, who is this?" Corrine asked, nudging her head at Niasia, who was growing more irate the closer she grew.

Niasia cocked her head to the side. "'Baby'? Oh, this is what we're doing today? Because I could've sworn last night I was way more than 'baby.'"

"Niasia," I warned, giving her a look that shut her down instantly. "This is my best friend, Corrine. Don't get yourself hurt in the middle of this store over someone fucking with you."

Corrine stuck her tongue out at Niasia. "Yup, I was just playing," she said, letting go of my hands and pointing to a rounder filled with panties. "I'll leave you to talk with *your friend* while I shop for some more stuff to wear to Jamaica. Toodles."

"Oh, that's a bold one," Niasia said, pointing to Corrine with a smirk on her face. "Your 'best friend' must not know how I get down when it comes to what's mine."

"You must not know that I don't belong to anybody," I countered, shoving my hands in my pocket. "When you see me out and about, if you can't keep it casual, then don't say anything at all."

Niasia looked apologetic. "But what if I wanna ask you to come over to my place tonight, and have some fun with me and my girl?"

My eyes wandered over to Niasia's friend, a thick redbone that was steadily playing with the lacy black teddy in her hand. "I might be able to do that."

"You know you want to, Quade," Niasia purred. "You can even bring your best friend with you. Me and my girl don't discriminate."

"Nah, Corrine is a good girl; she ain't going for no shit like this, and even if she was, she the homie. But I will see you later on."

Niasia puckered her lips at me. "'Kay."

Corrine had her face frowned up as I approached. She angrily flicked through the panties on the rounder, tossing some even. I gave her a playful nudge as if to ask her what was with the sudden change in her mood.

"Do I have to spell it out for you, Quade? I'm tired of being the 'good girl' and 'the homie.' We've grown up together and I'm sure you can see exactly how much I've *grown*."

I gave Corrine a thorough onceover, starting with her toned legs, thick thighs, fat ass, slim waist, decent titties, and admiring her beautiful face. With mock seriousness, I replied, "Hell nah: you look the same to me."

"Quade," Corrine whined.

"Seriously?" I said, placing a reassuring hand on her waist. "I think we're better as friends. The last thing I want is to complicate what we have. Other than my brothers, you're the only person I can talk to about whatever's going on in my life. I can't risk security like that over a relationship that might not even last."

"What if we're good together though? You ever think of that? I've known you since we were eight years old, and all I want is for us to give it a try." Corrine closed the distance between us. "Fuck your hoes tonight, but when we get on that plane to Jamaica tomorrow, can we give us a shot? If it doesn't work out by the end of the trip, I'll never bring it up again."

I shook my head. "Corrine, you're playing with fire..."

"Only because you're worth it."

It wasn't too long ago that I could see something popping off between Corrine and I, but ever since I met Yara, my mind had been changed. She was a little bratty, and got on my nerves with her faux bougie ass, but at some point unbeknownst to either of us, I woke up with her in my arms. I poised myself to push her away until I got a look at how peaceful she was as she slept. My heart wouldn't allow me to ruin her peace, so I lay there watching her for most of the morning, dejected when she rolled over to the other side of the bed. My body was still craving her warmth even after days of separation. If I couldn't have Yara, who had seen me at my realest, then I guess Corrine would be a nice runner up.

******

Corrine admired the private jet over the rim of her Cole Haan shades, staring excitedly between the plane and me. "Damn, you Townsend boys always have to be extra, don't you?"

"This is all Zeus' doing," I told her. "This nigga refuses to fly commercial. I don't see the difference between the two, but he's convinced that the experience is different."

"You're joking right?" Corrine asked, her expression hoping that I was. She handed me her phone, and begged, "Can you please take some pictures of me entering the jet. I want these hoes to eat their hearts out. While they're spending their weekend on the block doing basic shit, I'm going to be on the beaches of Jamaica."

I wasn't into all that social media bullshit, but Corrine was; she had spent the entire ride to the airport on Instagram, Snapchat, and telling the entire world of Facebook what she was up to. I had to stop her a few times from including me in any pictures or mentioning that I was the one she was with. I could only imagine how much niggas would act up if they found out that I was out of the country. She was in her feelings for a minute, and only seemed to understand where I was coming from after explaining that to her. That was a huge reason why I couldn't see us in a relationship; I needed my woman to follow my lead with no questions asked. Kind of like—

"Yara?" I said under my breath at the sight of Yara comfortably seated at one of the plane's windows.

Corrine must've heard me because her head snapped straight to Yara. "Lemme guess: when you asked me to pick up that outfit from last week, it was for her?"

"Not important," I said, traveling deeper into the private jet.

I dapped each one of my brothers on my way to the last row. They already knew no matter where we went I needed a lay of the land. I wanted to see the comings and goings of everyone onboard the flight, which was why being seated adjacent to the bathroom was always the best solution. Right off the bat, I could tell Corrine wasn't feeling it.

"Quade, we are on a plane with nothing but your brothers. Can you please tell me why you're being so paranoid?"

"Ain't nobody being paranoid; I'm just overly observant," I replied, settling into my seat. "You're more than welcome to sit somewhere else. I got some work to catch up on anyway."

Corrine looked like she didn't want to leave me, but she also didn't want to risk smelling the comings and goings of anyone who might use the bathroom. I nudged my head towards the shorty Savion was with and the conversation she was having with Hasani's girl, Gia. Corrine kissed me on the cheek and left to go have girl talk. Pulling out my notebook, I started looking over my notes to see if I could narrow down whoever stole our stash.

One of our lieutenants, Hampton, had been handling the drops for the past year without a hitch. Being that we dealt with a large amount of weight, Hampton had the bright idea of making the drops at different gyms around Brooklyn, where it wasn't out of the ordinary to come and leave with a duffle bag. For the past year and a half, it had been working without a hitch, until recently. Hampton was exiting the gym when niggas robbed him on his way to his car. I asked my supplier if he got caught with the cash, but he hadn't. This was either an inside job, or niggas had been watching harder than we initially thought.

"Look who finally made it," Hasani shouted as Savion whooped and whistled. "And who is that on your arm?"

Zeus came through looking like money in a clean white linen suit with a bad mamí on his arm. She was made up like a doll, and her dimensions were out of this world as well. Gia slapped Hasani on the arm for looking at shorty's fat ass a little too long, whereas Savion and his date were checking her out. *Looks like this nigga's met his match,* I thought with a laugh at the couple exchanging a glance and getting back to the conversation at hand. Corrine stole a peek in my direction to see if I was still looking, and knowing how sensitive she was, I spared her feelings by returning my attention to my notebook. This went on for half of the flight, with my thoughts straying to Yara every now and again. I heard her friend mention she wasn't feeling too well because of the pain pills she was on. What Yara was doing on pain pills ran through my mind until she finally got up to use the bathroom. I played it cool, keeping my attention on my notebook, patiently waiting for her to be finished. She didn't get a chance to pass my aisle before I snatched her into the seat beside me, careful not to grab the brace on her wrist.

"Good morning to you, too," she said, her eyes widening in shock as she nervously rubbed her wrist.

I nudged my head at it. "What happened to your wrist?"

"Nothing, I was doing some work at home, tripped over my rug, and fell on my wrist. It's no big deal," she said, her eyes darting around here and there.

"You sure this has nothing to do with the other night?" I questioned. "You should've told me your nigga got a hand problem; I would've handled it."

"Amir doesn't have a hand problem, and even if he did, he isn't my problem anymore. We broke up earlier this week."

"I hope it had nothing to do with me keeping you out," I lied, not the least bit sorry over her being done with whatever cornball ass nigga she was dealing with.

Yara shook her head. "No, that was one of the turning points for us, but it had nothing to do with me not being with him anymore. He was cheating on me…with my other best friend. Well, the bitch ain't my best friend no more."

"The one Zeus was messing with?"

"That's the one," Yara replied, biting her lip. "Bitch played the fuck out of me, her and Amir, but it's all good because I don't need either one of them. I lost it for a minute, but I've found my worth again. The next man will have to come correct or don't come at all."

There was nothing sexier in the world than listening to a woman speak on how much she loved herself. My moms would always preach to us how it was hard to expect others to care about you if you didn't give a fuck about yourself, and it was true. In my twenty-six years on this earth, I never had to do more than the bare minimum for these hoes because they never expected me to. I was able to get pussy at my leisure, and all it cost was a trip to Popeyes. Yara was already setting the tone for how I would treat her, and it was proving to be in a positive way.

"That's wassup," I said, fidgeting with the edge of my notebook. "Is that why you decided to come to Jamaica? Tryna get your groove back and shit?"

The sweetest laugh came from between Yara's lips. "Nah, I'm only coming to kick my feet up, smoke a blunt, have some local fun, and do me. There's more than enough time in the world for me to find someone else." Her eyes traveled to my notebook. "Was I interrupting your work?"

"Nah. Honestly, I can't even focus on it."

Yara held her hand out for the notebook. "You mind if I have a look? I might be able to help."

I never let anyone get a look at my strategy book. The last female to even flip to the first page damn near lost her fingers in the process. I took my work seriously, which was why I had no idea where the "sure" came from. Yara's eyes skimmed the location dates and drops, furrowing as she absorbed the information. A simple "huh" passed between her lips.

"What?" I said, leaning over to see what she saw.

"These are gyms, right?"

"Yeah..."

"Well, I work for a gym and we have regular clients all the time. They show up the same days of the week like clockwork, but never at the same time. I don't know what you're looking for, but I'm assuming that if it has to do with a security breach it could be because your meets are at the same time, at three different gyms. If someone wanted to find you it would be pretty easy."

"How easy?" I asked her.

"Your logins are kept track of. So if someone had access to the gym's database, they could easily track which gyms you visit and at what time. Once they know the pattern, they could do whatever they want."

"You tryna say that I might not even be looking for a regular street nigga? I might be looking for someone that works for the gym?"

"Find out who's at the gyms at that same time on those days, and you'll be able to narrow down the options," Yara said, closing the book. She held it out to me. "I hope I helped."

"You helped a whole lot. I owe you dinner," I said, the words tumbling out of my mouth. "Tonight after you're settled in."

Yara smiled, a genuine smile that stirred something deep inside of me. "I'd like that."

I accepted the book back from her, making sure to brush against her soft hands. She returned to her seat, catching looks from everyone along the way, the main one being Corrine, whose eyes followed her out of sight. I could tell she caught most of the conversation judging by the look on her face. A single tear fell from her eye, which she caught before it could even slide all the way down. It wasn't my intent to hurt her feelings, but Yara had me acting completely out of character. Inviting her into my world, making plans, and planning on keeping them. We hadn't even landed and I could tell this trip would be nothing but drama.

******

I stared down at the small mountain of clothes I had brought with me, trying to figure out how I would make this work. Corrine had picked out all of these outfits while I talked business on the phone and approved anything she put together. Now I was wishing I had paid her even an ounce of attention because with her not talking to me, I was on my own for tonight. I had pieced together a pair of white Ralph Lauren shorts with a white tee when there was a knock on my door. To my surprise, it was Yara's friend, Cash.

"Hey, can I talk to you for a minute?" she chirped, bobbing on her heels. "It's about Yara."

I opened the door wider. "Come in."

Cash cased the place, her eyes traveling around my junior suite. "The rest of the guys are in presidential suites…"

"My brothers know I don't like hotel rooms with multiple rooms. If some shit pops off I need to know there's only one entrance and exit. Plus, the view is nice down here," I added, trying not to reveal how paranoid I really am. "You came down here to make sure ya girl ain't going out with a psychopath? I'm not that crazy, I promise."

Cash laughed. "Was that a joke? You can be kinda funny when you wanna be."

"Mmmhmm," was all I could come up with because I wasn't

joking.

"Anyway, I came down here to let you know that my girl has been through a lot over this past week, and the last thing I want is for her state of mind to be taken advantage of. If you wanna get to know her, fine, but please don't make any promises you can't keep."

"I don't intend to."

"Good," Cash replied, nodding her head like she still had something else to say. She pointed to the outfit next to the pile of clothes on the bed. "Is that what you're wearing tonight?"

"Why, what's wrong with it?"

Cash glanced from the pile of clothes to me. "You have no idea how to put any of this together, do you?"

"I don't do any of this designer shit. I live in sweats, tees, comfortable sneakers—dassit."

Cash fingered the Versace shirt. "How about this? I'll put all of your outfits for the weekend together for you. I can't have you walking around with my girl looking crazy."

"Fine," I said taking a seat in a neighboring chair. "Do you."

I watched as Cash artfully put together all the clothes I had into a pretty decent wardrobe. I was set for breakfast, lunch, dinner, and everything in between. She told me which shoes were to go with what outfit, and her choices were better than the ones Corrine originally laid out.

"You a stylist or something?" I asked. "'Cause I can use someone back in the city to shop for me."

"I'm not a stylist, but I can be," she said excitedly. "Lemme know your budget, and I'll make it work."

"No budget; just pick out anything that'll make a nigga look good."

Cash danced towards the door. "That I can do. If you like what I did for you, wait until you see my girl. She's gonna be looking hella cute, so whatever you have planned, make sure it's good."

"Of course," I replied, with a mock salute.

I had been around my fair share of broads, and while most of them would come around on that "make sure you're good to my girl," none of them were ever as genuine as Cash coming down here to have a talk with me. Yara was loved by herself, and everyone on her team, so it was only right I kept up the tradition by making sure she was well taken care of.

******

"Damn," was the first word that came out of my mouth at the sight of Yara.

She was wearing the fuck out of a strappy white dress. On her feet were some punk furry shoes, revealing her pretty toes. I had a thing for pretty feet, and hers were perfect. She hid her brace with a pink Gucci scarf, which I thought was cute.

"I hope that's a good 'damn,'" Yara replied as she took in my outfit. "You clean up pretty nice yourself, Mr. Sweats. Your brothers were convinced that you would show up wearing a tee with some joggers and slippers, looking every part of an assassin. You proved them wrong in a very right way."

"When you're fucking with an underdog, you'll always have surprises like this," I told her, intertwining our arms and leading her down to the cabanas. "Enjoying the island so far?"

"Lunch with Cash and your brothers was cool. I have a question though."

"Shoot."

"The girl you got on the plane with...what's going on between the two of you?"

I shook my head. "Nothing. That's just Corrine; she's one of the homies."

"She ain't seem like much of a homie with the way she's been grilling me since we got here."

"Don't worry about her, ma. She's overprotective of me, like the sister I never had," I said dismissively. "Think about it: if she was my woman, would I be here with you, getting ready to eat some gourmet Jamaican food beachside?"

"No..."

"Okay then, relax, and let me spoil you a little," I said, shooting her a reassuring smile.

We arrived at a cabana I rented for the night. Inside was dinner set for two along with some wine and champagne. Yara was impressed; I could tell by the way she ran her hands over the linen tablecloth, and gave the bed in the corner a little test drive. Shit, if she wanted we could give it a thorough tryout and eat this food later. I had taken two steps towards her when she hopped off the bed, wagging her finger at me.

"I know what you were thinking, and that is not happening tonight, buddy," Yara chided as she slid into her seat. I pushed her in like a gentleman, using the opportunity to get a good look at her titties sitting pretty. "I came out to get to know you, so that's the plan for tonight. Tell me a little bit about yourself, Quade."

I plopped down into my chair with a bottle of wine in hand. As I poured us each a glass, I tried to think of something interesting to tell her about myself, but came up short. *Fuck it, she's already seen the real me,* I thought to myself after a lengthy pause.

"Um...my names Quade; I'm a Scorpio; I kill people for a living, mainly niggas that cross me and my family; I'm a hustler, and when I'm not killing niggas I'm typically getting money through my other business endeavors; My favorite food is Popeyes...what?"

Yara was sitting across from the table laughing at me. She wiped away tears from her eyes. "I'm sorry, I just...I never would've imagined in a million years that my first date after breaking up with my boyfriend would be with a professional killer."

"Are you regretting it?" I asked.

Yara shook her head. "Not really."

"Good. 'Cause I'm a regular guy that does regular things—"

"When you're not killing people inside of the women's restroom at a nightclub," Yara said with a wink.

It was at that moment that I knew shorty was different. Yara didn't shrink away from me like some of the broads I used to deal with, and she wasn't drawn to me because of what I had to offer. Some bitches heard the Townsend name and automatically thought I would be their come up; you could imagine their disappointment when all I did was get the pussy and head for the door. I had more babies pinned on me than I cared for, none of which proved to be my kids because there was no way I could strap up for combat on the streets and not when it came to fucking with a bitch I wasn't exclusive with. I didn't get that treacherous vibe from Yara, and for that reason alone I was able to open up to her completely.

"This wasn't bad for my first date ever," I said as I brought Yara back to her room. "I can think of a way it would be better...but we ain't gotta do all of that," I finished at the look on Yara's face.

Yara's eyes widened. "Quade, you're not seriously telling me that you've never been on a date."

"I never had a reason to; when women throw the pussy at you with no expectations, you take it. This is the first time I've ever went through this much effort to take a woman out. Reminds me of when my pops would take my moms out every Friday night," I reminisced. "I had a nice time with you, Yara."

"So did I, Quade," Yara replied, leaning against her door. "I hope we can do this again."

I leaned in and planted a gentle kiss on her lips, savoring the taste of champagne on her lips. She became surprisingly aggressive, pressing herself against me, and running her hands through my hair. I picked her up in one swoop, placing her against the door, ready to get it in right there in the hallway when she stopped me.

"I...um...I should get to bed," she stammered, tapping my shoulder so I could put her down. She fumbled with her purse, nearly dropping all of her personal items rushing to find her card key. She shoved it into the door and was in her room seconds later. "See you tomorrow at breakfast."

The door slammed shut, scaring the shit out of me. I don't know what Yara was hiding, but I would find out.

Cash

"Whoever taught you how to roll a blunt needs to be pistol whipped," Savion said with a laugh. "Cash, gimme the blunt before you make it fall apart."

I rolled out of Savion's reach while managing to keep my haphazardly rolled blunt in place. "No, I know what I'm doing, I promise. Lemme finish."

Savion reached out and pulled me across the king-sized bed of his presidential suite, only stopping when we were so close that our lips almost touched. "You better not waste a single drop of my weed, or that's your ass, Cash."

"A'ight, I got you." I rolled onto my stomach and added the finishing touches to the blunt, giving it a few thorough licks to make sure it was properly sealed. I noticed Savion had grown eerily silent. "What?"

"Nothing," he said, his eyes following my tongue up and down the blunt. "I'm just thinking that you might not be good at rolling a blunt, but you might be good at blowing something else."

I slapped him playfully on the arm. "Savion, you're disgusting!"

Savion used that as leverage to roll me onto my back and climb on top of me. I don't know if it was Jamaica, the liquor we had been drinking, the heat and smell of Savion's Issey Miyake cologne tickling my nose, or the fact that I hadn't had sex in a month, but if Savion didn't get off of me he was about to put in some work.

"What do you think you're doing?" I asked, pretending to squirm, but I was really using my leg to see what he was working with, and my leg was pleasantly surprised.

Savion laughed huskily. "You keep on moving like that and you'll find out."

"Oh really?" I countered, spreading my legs so he fell right between them. "Why don't you stop making empty threats, and show me what you're all about."

Savion leaned in and kissed me with an authority I had been missing since my relationship with Vito had gone to shit. I tossed the blunt aside, and grabbed the back of his head, running my hands through his thick, curly hair. This was one of the most intense make out sessions I had ever had, and Savion made it that much better when he rose up off of me to strip. He pulled his shirt over his head, revealing a set of lickable chocolate abs. I ran my hands over them, tracing my nails through each ridge until I reached the buckle of his belt. My mouth was already watering in anticipation as I unbuckled his Hermes belt, and I was nearly beside myself when I unzipped his pants, gasping at the bulge in his Frigo boxers.

"You sure you wanna unleash the beast?" Savion asked, placing his hands gently on top of mine.

I answered with a growl. Savion removed his hands, raising them in the air as I got to work. Savion's dick sprang from his boxers, standing at attention. It was pretty—the perfect shade of brown with veins traveling through it. I licked my lips and placed them on the head of his dick, moaning in delight at the taste of him. That small taste wasn't enough; I wanted it all in my mouth at once. I shoved Savion onto his back, earning a grunt of surprise from him that quickly changed to a moan when I devoured his dick.

"Shit," he hissed between his teeth as he lifted his head to watch the show down below. "I'mma need that weak ass blunt you rolled after this. Fuck!"

I let a small trail of spit fall out of my mouth and onto the head of his dick and used it to deliver one artful stroke after the next. I took that as affirmation that I was doing my thing and took this as an opportunity to take care of his boys. My hands never lost their rhythm as I sucked on his balls, juggling them in my mouth, and working my way back up to the head. There was never a man who could make it through one of my infamous blowjobs for more than ten minutes, but I'll be damn if Savion ain't last longer than the rest. For that reason, I wanted to end it right.

"Get up and fuck my mouth," I panted, getting on all fours.

Savion did as he was told, hitting my mouth with slow strokes before picking up the pace. I kept up with his rhythm, sucking and slurping until he exploded in my mouth. Not one to let anything go to waste, I swallowed every last drop, which earned a look of approval from Savion.

"You keep sucking a nigga dick like that, and whatever you want is yours," he laughed shakily. His phone buzzed from the head of the bed. "That's the call from the Jamaicans. I gotta handle this right now, but I promise when I get back I got you, ma. Order whatever you want."

"I wanna come," I said, following him into the bathroom, where he was freshening up. "I won't ask any questions, make any sudden movements, nothing. I'll be as quiet as a church mouse."

"My brothers aren't going for that," Savion replied. "Especially not Zeus. He would have a fit if I brought a liability along."

"Why I gotta be a liability?"

"Because if some shit pops off, I'm responsible for you. How am I supposed to explain to your people that you came out the country and got popped?"

"You don't have to do that because my mother is dead, my father didn't stay around long enough to even see me be born, and my boyfriend hasn't even noticed that I left. The only person who will give a fuck is Yara." I put on my puppy dog pout. "Please?"

"Why you even wanna go? You tryna get into the game?"

I shrugged. "Maybe."

Savion gave himself a once over in the mirror. He looked good, but the aftershocks of that soul sucking could be seen in his eyes, which found mine through the mirror, and replied, "A'ight. You got five minutes to be ready."

I used all five of my minutes to fix my hair, brush my teeth, and freshen up while Savion talked on the phone with his brothers. He hadn't mentioned me at any point of the conversation, so I knew he was banking on bringing me as a surprise in the hopes that everyone would buckle and let me come. I practiced my sad face on the walk to the car, hoping I could evoke some sympathy from the Townsend Brothers gathered by a Cadillac Escalade.

I might as well tried to get some sympathy from a rock.

"What the fuck is she doing here?" Quade asked off the bat. He was still wearing his outfit from his date with Yara, which made it hard for me to take him serious wearing a pair of black Armani trousers with a matching silk shirt. "I hope we dropping her off somewhere, Savion, 'cause shorty ain't riding to the meet. That's what we're not doing tonight."

"Yo, she can sit in the car," Savion said, wrapping a protective arm around my shoulder. "I promise she won't be any trouble, right Cash?"

"I promise to be on my best behavior. Right hand to God," I added, raising my right hand for emphasis.

Quade turned to Hasani, who replied, "Ever since we lost Mom it's always been the four of us. The only time we've ever considered letting a woman see how we handle business was if she's getting ready to become part of the family." His eyes flickered to me for a second. "Is that where this is going?"

"You gon' put me on the spot like that, Hasani?"

"You put us on the spot with an extra passenger," he countered. "So...what's going on here?"

I smiled up at Savion. "I don't want to you have to commit to anything you aren't ready for. I'll head back to the hotel and—"

"It's serious between the two of us."

"On ya Glock?" Quade countered.

"I swear on my Glock it's serious. Now come on before we show up late," Savion replied. He stopped short. "What, Zeus? You ain't say shit. What's on your mind?"

I thought Zeus was going to answer Savion, but instead he turned his attention to me. "You ever fired a gun?"

I nodded my head. "Way back in the day."

"Good. Hold this," he said, reaching in his waistband and handing me a Beretta. "Everyone on this team has a job. I'm the boss, Hasani's the bank, Savion is the transporter, and Quade is—"

"The one with the gun," Quade replied with a smile, revealing a set of perfect, white teeth. "Take that gun and lemme see if you know how to hold it. I ain't gon' have you as part of my backup and you can't even hold a gun."

I accepted the gun from Zeus and took the gun apart, making sure to clear the chamber. I put it back together and aimed straight ahead. "Is that good enough for you?"

"It'll do on such short notice."

I rolled my eyes at Quade's dramatic ass, but that didn't stop me from hopping into the front with Savion while Quade and two soldiers sat in the back. Hasani and Zeus took off in a separate SUV with two soldiers of their own. Savion turned the radio to a station playing laidback reggae music. I danced in my seat, wining my waist to the beat as I grinded into the plush leather seats of the Cadillac Escalade. Savion stole a peek or two from the corner of his eye, causing him to swerve every now and again.

"A nigga already not used to driving on this side of the road.

You gon' fuck around and have us in a ditch or something," Savion joked, laughing as I stuck my tongue at him. His smile dropped when he caught one of the soldiers peeking at me. "Nigga, you looking to end up in a fucking ditch tonight?! Look at my girl one more time and watch how quick I pull this car over and have you explain yourself to my nine."

"Nah, I wasn't looking at shorty," the guy replied apologetically, vehemently shaking his head. "I got a lazy eye is all."

"You need me to come back there and straighten that bitch?"

"Nah, nah, I'mma get it fixed."

"Get it fixed real soon before I fix it for you."

I usually didn't like being the source of negative attention, but I couldn't help how moist my panties got from Savion checking his nigga for looking at me. I couldn't count on my fingers the number of times that one of Vito's boys would eye me with no shame, and he'd claim as long as they only looked there wasn't a problem. That was all the permission those niggas needed to keep treating me like I was a piece of meat. I lost all respect for Vito that day, and only stayed for what he brought to the table. Being here with Savion was enough to have me reconsider my relationship as a whole. I spent the rest of the ride replaying the scene with a small smile on my face. Quade stared at me with thinly veiled disapproval, shaking his head as we pulled up to the rendezvous point inside of a warehouse.

"You don't go anywhere," Quade said, hopping into the driver's seat as Savion hopped out of the SUV, the two soldiers flanking him. "I told you you're here as backup. Roll down your window and just listen."

"So you mean we don't even get to be part of the meet?"

"No…how can we be part of the meet and watch my brothers at the same time? This ain't no glamorous shit; one mistake can easily have someone end up dead."

I rolled my eyes. "Has anyone ever told you that you're paranoid? Like are you on something?"

"I ain't on shit, aight? I'm just sick and tired of burying people that mean something to me because someone slipped up and didn't pay attention. So shut up and keep watch," Quade snapped.

I would've snapped back at him had I not heard the pain underneath that sullen tone of his. Knowing how his parents were killed also gave me the patience most lack. I sat back in my seat with my gun on my lap, my finger on the trigger, waiting for something, anything to pop off.

"So those are the Jamaicans?" I asked, my eyes widening at the appearance of three handsome men and a beautiful woman. "Who is she and how does she get to go to the meeting but I can't?"

"That's Moe. Moe is married to Onyx, the nigga next to her wearing a suit. Him and Zeus get along real well; he claims he was introduced to Onyx at one of his nightclubs, but you can't tell me them niggas ain't meet at Men's Warehouse, or wherever they buy all these fucking suits from," Quade said with a trace of disinterest. "Moe is there because she's a business partner that put in work. Shorty ain't just slide her way into the operation; from what I've been told, she started as a soldier."

Taking one look at the gorgeous Moe, who was dressed in a black leather jacket with skintight jeans and a pair of Saint Laurent combat boots, it was hard to believe she started from the bottom of anything. She might've been bad—with her perfect hourglass figure, rich cocoa skin, and slick ponytail—but when I saw the two Glocks underneath her jacket I knew she had to be just as lethal as her man.

"Well she's certainly about her business," I said, watching as Moe and Onyx talked business with Zeus and Hasani. "I wanna be like her when I grow up."

Quade scoffed. "You got a long way to go, ma."

I was mid-eye roll when I caught something moving out the corner of my eye. "Quade, did you see that?"

"Hell yeah," he said, placing the car in drive. "I need to you grab the wheel and guide while I drive. Can you do that?"

"Yeah…"

Quade picked up a walkie and spoke into it. "Zeus, fall back. It's an ambush."

No sooner had Quade spoken the words did shots ring out. Everyone sprung into action. Zeus, Hasani, and Savion reacted at the same time as Moe, Onyx, and their soldiers. Everyone withdrew their guns and hit the unknown enemies with heavy fire. Quade whipped out two guns of his own, spread his arms wide and gunned it straight into the thick of the battle, popping off shots at the dark figures that appeared from the bushes. I watched as soldiers dropped like flies while the three Townsend Brothers held their own. The always pretty Zeus resembled a monster as he fired off shots from both Smith & Wesson's in his hand. Savion flanked him as he crept towards the first car, slid in, and revved the engine. Hasani jumped into the car as well, along with two of the remaining soldiers. The gunmen disappeared as fast as they came, straight into the woods.

"Put it in reverse and let's get out of here," Quade commanded, dropping his magazines and reloading. "Them niggas ran scared or they want me to fuck around and run after them."

I put the car in reverse and gunned it out of the rendezvous point. Only once we were clear did Quade put his guns away and take the wheel. I sat back in my seat, chest heaving, heart pumping, back sweating, and hands shaking. Quade glanced over at me with a large smile on his face. Of course his crazy ass would think this was cool.

"You good?"

"I…I think so."

"You alive so the answer should be 'yes.' I don't normally tell people this but…you did well for your first gunfight. By the next one you won't even shake anymore," he said in what was supposed to be an encouraging tone, but I could barely hear him over my heart beating in my ears. "I remember mine. Took out three niggas but one of them clipped me on the shoulder. It was all good though; I only had to miss a couple days of class."

"I didn't know you went to college."

"College? That's for people with a future. I'm talking about middle school."

I snapped my head at him. "Nigga, what?"

"What?" Quade echoed with a hint of confusion.

My phone buzzed in my pocket, scaring the shit out of me. I picked up on the second buzz with a breathless, "Hello?"

"Yo, you good?" Savion asked with no preamble. "Had I known niggas would pop off like that I would've never brought you along."

"I'm okay; Quade and I handled it."

"Aight, I'll see you when we get back to the hotel."

I relaxed in my seat, taking deep breaths until I fell asleep. I woke up to the balmy night air washing over my skin followed by Savion pressing a kiss against my lips. My eyes fluttered open, drinking in how worried he was about me. We had only known each other for a week and here he was, looking at me like we had been together for years. He held me in his arms and I knew that was where I wanted to be.

Yara

After my amazing date with Quade, you could imagine my disappointment when Cash came to my room telling me we had to go home. I was sitting at the edge of the bed confused as hell, watching as she packed my bags for me. I flinched at the sweats and hoodie she tossed in my direction. By the time I had changed clothes, she was zipping up my luggage.

"Cash, what the fuck is going on?" I asked, rubbing my eyes as we dashed through the hotel. "One minute we're living it up and the next we're back on a flight to New York? Did something happen during the three hours I went to sleep."

Cash glanced back at me. "You wouldn't believe me if I told you."

"Try me."

"I'll let you know on the plane."

Zeus, Savion, and the other two women were in the hotel lobby with their bags. Zeus was calming his girl down as she frantically asked him what was going on. Quade's friend, Corrine, stood off to the side of the couple, switching between looking around and texting on her phone. At the sight of us, she rolled her eyes and went back to texting. She had been giving me attitude ever since we got off the plane.

"Ladies, the jet is gassed up and waiting. We'll be back tomorrow.

Melissa," Zeus said, holding the crying woman by her chin. "Calm down. Everything is going to be alright."

"Zeus, what if something had happened to you? I thought I could deal with this, but obviously I can't. Make it back safe, but I'll see you around."

Zeus gave a nonchalant shrug, watching her trudge out of the hotel to the Mercedes Benz van waiting for us. "Same here."

I shrugged my duffle bag a little higher on my shoulder. Zeus noticed my slight struggle and took the bag from me. He surprised me by taking the handle to my rolling luggage too. "You look like you could use a little help with that messed up wrist."

"Yeah. I would've asked Cash but she brought along her whole wardrobe for a weekend vacation," I said, nudging my head to Cash, who was carrying her purse and Louis Vuitton duffle while Savion carried the matching suitcase in one hand while rolling the luggage in the other.

"Sorry it had to end like this before y'all got to enjoy the rest of the island. I might throw together a non-work trip in the future. Would you be interested in coming along?"

My brows disappeared into my bandanna. "Is it a group trip?"

"Of course," Zeus replied, but I wasn't too sure if I should believe him. "It'll be slightly more intimate, but a group trip nonetheless."

"Okay then. I'll come out for another trip. We had fun hanging out earlier today," I replied, slipping into the van last. "Thanks for the help, Zeus. Can you tell Quade I'll see him back in New York?"

"I got you," Zeus said with a smile as he closed the door for me.

"Make sure to call as soon as the plane touches back down in New York," Savion called out as the car pulled off.

"We will," we chimed.

The car had barely left the hotel driveway when Corrine started her shit. Melissa was sitting directly behind me crying her eyes out and mumbling that she wasn't built for the lifestyle. Cash sat there rolling her eyes, mouthing "blah, blah, blah" the entire time as I silently laughed. The interaction flew right over Melissa's head, but not Corrine. She had to use the small exchange to fuel her hate.

"To make it even worse, I feel like Zeus didn't even give a fuck about how I felt. I wanted him to at least hold me or drive with us to the airport to make sure we got on the plane safe."

Cash scoffed. "If you were present for what he had been through only hours before, you wouldn't be sitting here talking all of that shit. Zeus or any of the other brothers didn't come along because they need to act quickly before whoever tried to kill them tries again, hence why we're being sent back to America."

"At what point was your opinion asked?" Corrine countered, frowning up her face in contempt. "You go on one ride-along with the Townsend Brothers and all of a sudden you're an authority on how they do business?"

"You haven't been on one yet so that makes me more of an authority than you," Cash shot back. She tossed her purse to the side and angled herself to where she could pounce if need be. "Like I said, I'm sure Zeus would've came along if it wouldn't have been a danger to us."

"I know," Melissa cried. "I'm just being emotional because this has never happened to me before. I'll call him when we reach New York and try to do some damage control."

"If it ain't too late. Someone's being a little greedy. I guess one Townsend brother isn't enough..."

"Excuse me?" I said, catching the shade Corrine threw with no shame. "I know you're not talking about me. Zeus saw me struggling, and like any decent man with manners, helped me with my stuff. That's all it was, but this is starting to feel like it has something to do with Quade taking me out to dinner tonight."

"You know what? It does. Whether he knows it or not, I'm what Quade needs. I have been looking out for him since we were kids. Defending him against the kids that called him weird, protecting the kids that called him weird from his wrath, and being the only person in his life to accept him for who he is," Corrine said, her voice starting to choke up. "Can you sit here and say that you commit to that?"

"Listen, I just got out of my own complicated relationship and—"

"That's what I thought," Corrine said, sinking back into her seat and staring out the window.

Cash gave her the stank face and turned back to me. "Girl, pay her no mind. Obviously she came here to get some island dick she didn't receive, so she wants to take it out on you."

Cash was absolutely right; Quade wasn't making all of these demands from me so why should I have to answer to his friend? I shoved Corrine's insecure ramblings to the side and focused on making plans for when I got back to New York, which were to find somewhere to live, heal my broken heart, and focus on loving myself again.

******

"Yes, we touched down safe," Cash said into her phone as we climbed into a taxi at the airport. She glanced over at me. "Yara's safe and sound as well. I'll see you when you get back, okay? Okay, bye."

I stared at Cash's phone and back at her. "Someone's in love."

"Ugh, I'm not in love, I'm just really feeling Savion more than I thought I would. Have you ever met someone that you just clicked with once you got to know them?"

I thought of my dinner with Quade. "Yeah..."

"So then you know exactly what I'm talking about. Savion is different than any other guy I've dealt with. Lately I've been feeling like I'm not doing enough to secure my future, and instead of brushing me off, Savion is helping me find myself."

Cash was practically glowing as she praised Savion. I could see that it was genuine on his part as well, which made it easy for me to say, "Follow your heart, Cash. Any man that can have you smiling and thinking about getting a job is cool with me. It's nice to see he's making such a strong impression on you."

"Speaking of strong impressions...I think you might've made one on Zeus. Savion said he wanted to know if you were good. I only got into homegirl back there because I could feel the hate coming off of her, but she's right; I think you've got the attention of two Townsend Brothers."

I did recall Zeus' vivid description of me the night I was with Quade. He thought that I was prettier than Sharise, which was something I would've never expected from a man of Zeus' caliber. Normally men ogled Sharise and treated me like the cute friend you might settle for if she wasn't interested. For Zeus to see me as me and not as a runner up was kind of…flattering. Cash studied the look on my face.

"You like him back?"

"Of course not. I'm kinda interested in Quade."

"You mean Quade that hasn't even called to make sure you're good?"

"I can't take that too personally. Something tells me that Quade isn't used to checking up on women and whatnot."

Cash nodded in agreement. "True, true. But you should weigh your options before writing off one brother over the other. Zeus is a god: he's handsome, wealthy, stylish as fuck, and if the rumors are true, he's packing. Whereas Quade is…"

"Quade is what?"

"Bat shit crazy. I mean he seems like a decent guy, but he's damaged, Yara. After everything you've been through with Amir, you need someone that can treat you right without the added headache."

I recalled the wonderful date I had with Quade, and told Cash, "I know he's a little damaged, partially crazy, and a little eccentric, but he's also real. I've been missing something real from my life for a really long time."

Of course everyone got the paranoid Quade that was walking around with several chips on his shoulder, but deep down on the inside I knew there was a broken man looking to be loved.

"Look at that smile on your face. Seems like you're really liking him, which is strange because didn't you two meet on the plane? How did a ten minute conversation turn into a love connection?"

I was spared from having to answer as the cabbie shouted, "Which building?"

"Keep going...keep going...right here. Thanks," Cash said, rummaging through her purse for cash. I beat her to the punch by swiping my credit card on the little keypad in the back. "Yara, I'm the one that invited you—"

"And you're also the one letting me stay at your place free of charge. If you wanna even it out you can help me with my bags."

"Girl, I can barely help myself with my bags. Lemme grab Vito so he can bring all of these bags in," Cash replied, hopping out and making her way up the stairs of the immaculate brownstone.

I started taking them out of the trunk with the help of the cabbie. We had placed the remaining bags on the sidewalk when Cash came back outside looking shook. I tipped the cabbie twenty to get him going so I could find out what's wrong with my girl. Cash came rushing down the stairs in one shoe, nearly killing herself in the single six-inch heel.

"I need you to go upstairs, go in my bedroom, and hide everything on the bed. Please," she whispered. "I gotta make a phone call."

The look on my girl's face told me to save the questions for later. I raced upstairs and into the apartment. The living room was a complete mess: couch cushions were strewn all over, shoes littered the floor, and liquor bottles were strewn haphazardly all over. I delved deeper into the house, and it became glaringly obvious that Vito had a party while we were gone. I stopped in my tracks at the sight of him sprawled out in the bed with a woman beside him. His chest rose and fell steadily, which was the opposite of the woman beside him. A brick of coke sat between them.

"Oh shit," I said, grabbing the kilo and trying to think on my feet.

I entered the closet and nearly dropped dead myself at the sight of Cash's wardrobe. Rows of clothes and racks of shoes lined the closet. If the police were on their way like I suspected, this didn't need to be in plain sight. I stood on a stool and grabbed one of Vito's sneaker boxes. I popped it open and nearly fainted when I spotted another kilo perfectly wrapped up with the red devil stamp on its center smiling at me menacingly.

"This nigga can't be serious," I muttered as I placed the coke into the shoebox and placed it back where I found it.

Cash was sitting in the living room with her head in her hands, shaking with sobs. I sat beside her and took her into my arms, rocking her back and forth trying to comfort her the best I could.

"Everything's going to be okay," I whispered in her ear. "They're going to come and ask us some questions and we'll answer as honestly as we can, okay. It's an overdose so this should be pretty open and shut."

"This isn't the first time it's happened," Cash admitted between sobs. "The other day I caught him—"

There was a knock at the front door as the EMTs entered the

apartment. Cash rose from her seat and took them into the bedroom. The police followed shortly after, asking questions the second they crossed the threshold. We had nothing to hide, which made answering their questions pretty easy. Our luggage was also an indicator that we had nothing to do with the situation. We were absolved of any wrongdoing due to the Good Samaritan Fatal Overdose law. I choked back a sob at the sight of the body bag leaving the apartment.

"Have a good night, Officer," Cash choked out, closing the door behind her. She leaned against it and slid to the floor, sobbing on the way down. "I can't believe this shit is happening all over again. How could he fucking do this to me again?"

"Cashmere," Vito said from the kitchen doorway. He was holding on to every stable fixture within an arm's reach to get to her. "Cash, stop crying. I swear I ain't know that was gon' happen. I took a nap and shorty must've had more than she could handle. I told her not to go dipping without my supervision and—"

"Are you fucking serious right now?" Cash asked in a deadly whisper. She fumbled to her feet and shouted, "ARE YOU FUCKING SERIOUS RIGHT NOW VITO?! THERE WAS A DEAD WOMAN IN OUR BED!"

"Cash, calm down before the neighbors hear—"

"You're worried about them hearing when they can see the dead woman leaving our apartment?" Cash paced the living room, shaking her head as she grabbed fistfuls of hair. She spun around in time to catch Vito nodding off. "What the fuck is wrong with you, Vito? Coke doesn't make you lean. That's not all you've been getting into, is it?

You're back to fucking with that other shit."

"Listen, Cash, you ain't my mother. You don't get to talk to me any old way and—"

"And what? Vito, I had to come home and once again clean up your shit. What if they would've came in here and saw what was on the bed? You'd be back in jail doing time, but I'm starting to think that's where you need to be because at the rate you're going…you won't make it to the end of the year." Cash went from angry to tired and hurt. "Vito, I can't do this anymore. I cannot continue to be your crutch. You're going to be the death of me."

"So that's it? You just gon' give up on me when shit gets tough? I thought you were different from these other bitches, but I guess I was wrong."

"Vito, you need help," Cash urged, walking up to him and holding his face. "You need to go to rehab and get some help."

"I don't need rehab!"

"You laid in bed next to a dead woman for hours and didn't even know, Vito. How much longer is it going to take where I'm lying in bed and you're the dead one? My heart can't take it." Vito sunk into her arms, his body shaking with sobs. "If you can't do it for yourself, Vito, please do it for me."

"Okay," Vito cried. "I'll go, but only for you."

With the help of Cash, Vito took a shower, got dressed, and packed a small suitcase. I offered to stay behind and clean up while Cash took Vito to an inpatient rehab. As I put the house back in order, my mind wandered to Quade and what he was possibly up to. I wanted to call him, but I didn't want to look desperate. My phone buzzed at the thought, and I almost thought God was answering my prayers until I saw who it was.

"Hello, Amir, what can I do for you?" I asked drily as I took a seat at the edge of Cash's now spotless bedroom.

"I miss you, Yara."

I scoffed. "It took you how many days to come to that conclusion?"

"I missed you from the moment you walked out the door, but I knew you had to take some time away from me so you could cool off."

"Cool off because my pussy was burning. And why is my pussy burning? Oh, yeah, because you started cheating on me with other women. Amir, do you know how dangerous what you did was? What if it wasn't Trich? What if it was something worse?"

"I know, Yara. I fucked up and I'm sorry. I'm sorry for everything I said, I'm sorry for fucking women in our bed, I'm sorry for one of the women being your best friend. If you give me another chance I swear I'll do right by you."

I shook my head although he couldn't see me. "No, Amir. I'm not giving you another chance to step all over my heart. You had me, a good woman that loved you with all her heart, and you did me wrong."

"That's how it is?" Amir countered. "That's how you wanna play this?"

"Yes, that's exactly how I'm playing this."

"Fine. I ain't want your weak ass back anyway. What type of stupid bitch listens to her man fuck another woman and does nothing about it?"

"The same stupid kind of bitch you wanted to be with thirty seconds ago," I said, laughing at the audacity of this nigga. "Now do me a favor and have my keepsake box right at the front door tomorrow so I can pick it up."

"You'll get your keepsake box when I feel like it."

"Amir—"

The call ended before I could get another word in edgewise. I was gearing up to call him back when the front door opened and in walked Cash. She looked worse for wear: her hair was in a fuzzy halo around her head, her makeup was smudged from her crying, and I could see the hurt in her eyes.

"He's going to be in for ninety days," Cash announced, taking a seat next to me. "You should've seen him when they were escorting him away, Yara. He was staring at me like I betrayed him or something, when all I was trying to do was make sure he didn't end up dead..."

"I know, hun. He's mad at you right now, but when he gets clean and sees how much you helped him, he'll be thanking you."

Cash ran a hand through her hair. "Let's hope so." She rested her head against my shoulder. "Yara, I can't believe I let my life get to this point all for the sake of living a fabulous lifestyle."

"I can't believe I let mine be reduced to me staying for a man I knew fell out of love with me a long time ago."

"We just some tragic bitches, huh?"

"We are, but it doesn't matter as long as we got each other's backs.

If this is rock bottom then all we have to go from here is up."

"Facts," Cash replied, dapping me up. "To the come up?"

"To the come up."

Cashmere

I spent the rest of the night tossing and turning on the pullout bed I shared with Yara. Every time I slipped into even the slightest slumber, I was woken up by images of the dead woman in my bed. Dried vomit caked her lips, a bright contrast against her beautiful brown skin. I wasn't sure who she was, but I knew she was likely to be missed, and unfortunately, her people might come looking for Vito. These were the thoughts that ran through my head on a loop, over and over again until the sun finally came up. My lids drooped, and I was finally asleep when there was a knock at my door. I bolted upright, scaring Yara half to death.

"Shit," I muttered under my breath as I swung my legs over the edge of the bed. "It might be the police asking some follow up questions."

Three more knocks sounded throughout the living room. I slipped into my robe, making sure it was tied tight before opening the door. Imagine my annoyance to find my landlord standing there with a tight smile on his face. I opened the door wide enough for him to enter.

"Good morning, Mr. Brooks. I take it you're here because of what happened last night. I'm sure one of your *tenants* told you all about it, huh?" I said, saying the word exactly how it made my ass itch.

Mr. Brooks, an older white man with a permanent impassive

face, gave my bare legs and silk robe a thorough once-over. "That's one of the reasons why I'm here, Cashmere. This is your boyfriend's third incident this week. First, it was the music. Then the arguing at all times of the day and night. Now there are dead people being wheeled out of my building? And on top of that, you're past due on your rent for the second month in a row."

"Past due? That impossible; Vito might have his ways, but if there's one thing he's always done, it's pay our bills on time."

Mr. Brooks dug around in his pocket and came up with his phone. "Oh really...Then how do you explain this?" he asked as he tapped the phone screen and shoved it into my face. "What does that say?"

"'*Mr. Brooks you know I would never play you, especially since my girl loves living here so much. I promise to have the five grand to you by next month.*'" My heart sunk at the sight of Vito's current number right at the top of the message. "Mr. Brooks—"

"I'm done with the excuses, Cashmere," Mr. Brooks said, pocketing his phone. "You've already used up your security deposit, which makes you officially behind one month. You have exactly one week to have the back rent and replace your deposit, or you're out of here."

"I'll have the money to you by the end of the week. I promise," I said, although I had absolutely no idea how I was going to come up with five grand that quick.

Mr. Brooks knew I was lying out of my ass, but that didn't stop him from replying, "I hope for your sake that you do. If not, you'll find yourself and your belongings out on the street. Good day, Ms. Parker."

Mr. Brooks let himself out, leaving me standing there looking stupid. I plopped down on the couch bed next to Yara, who was watching me from underneath the blankets. Embarrassment tinged my cheeks red; I promised my girl a place to stay and now I wasn't even sure whether or not I would still be staying here. This was the moment when those life skills I was supposed to have came into play.

"I can't fucking believe he did this," I cried into my hands, still too ashamed to look at Yara. "I trusted him to handle everything and now look at my life. What the fuck am I supposed to do?"

"You can stop crying," Yara said, slinging her arm around me. "Listen, I have three grand saved. I planned on using it to put down on an apartment, but you can have it, Cash. I know you would do the same for me if I needed it."

"Yara, I can't take your money. You worked too damn hard for it."

"At my job, which I still have, so trust me when I say I can always go make some more."

"Not with your messed up wrist."

"I have plenty of vacation days I can cash in on. Let me help you out, Cash."

I stole a glance at her. "Okay, I have three grand; where will I get the other two from?"

"Have you not seen your closet? I'm sure you can sell a Fendi bag or two on the low with no problem. Ten pairs of your shoes at two hundred bucks a pop is the money right there."

"Two hundred dollars? Some of my shoes are worth five times

that amount."

"Well we don't have time to get those other four times, now do we? Or do you have something else of value that you think you can sell?"

A light bulb went off in my head. "I do have something else to sell. Yara…where did you put the snow?"

"Cash!" Yara's eyes widened in horror. "I know you're not considering what I think you are."

"Yara, the money would be too quick for me to pass up on. I can make at least $80,000 if I sell it."

"Or you could get caught and end up in jail for the rest of your life."

"Yara—"

"Cash," Yara said, grabbing me by the shoulders. "You are so much better than selling drugs. It would break my heart into pieces if you fucked around and got caught up in some more of Vito's bullshit. Take my money, sell a bag or two, and leave all this shit alone."

I felt another stream of tears fall before I could stop them. "Yara, you just don't get it, do you? You're the pretty girl that grew up with a mother who loved her, and who also told her that she could be anything. I wasn't given that luxury. I'm not as smart as you, not nearly as ambitious, and an honest living is something that I know nothing about. As my best friend you should be able to understand and respect it."

"I can't." Yara kissed me on the cheek. "I'll find a hotel to stay in until I get back on my feet. When you're ready to stop being scared of making a change, give me a call."

I watched as Yara got herself together extra slow, giving me as much time as she could to change my mind. She could've literally took a nap in between and we would still be stuck right at this crossroad. There was nothing she could say or do to change my mind.

"I'll talk to you later, Cash. Love you," Yara said as she wheeled her suitcase out of the front door.

"Love you too, Yara," I replied, blowing her an air kiss.

The sound of the closing door reverberated throughout the house, reminding me of exactly how alone I was in this entire situation. I lay back on the couch bed, staring up at the ceiling as I plotted my next move. I didn't have a clientele, I wasn't sure how the corner boys would take to me, and Yara was right: what if I got caught by the cops? These were the thoughts that plagued my mind, only stopping at the knock at my door. Imagine my surprise when I saw Sarah standing there looking worse for wear: her hair was all over her head, her clothes were disheveled, and she had that fiend look in her eyes.

"Hey, Cashmere," she said bobbing on her heels as she tried peeking behind me. "Is Vito home? I need to ask him something."

"Vito won't be home for a while. He had a family emergency out of town. Is there something I can help you with?" I asked, trying best to play dumb like she wasn't fiending for a toke.

"If you know where I can get some candy I would really appreciate it," she said, placing emphasis on the word. In a lower voice she added, "I've got cash."

"Come in. Maybe I can help you scratch that itch."

I welcomed Sarah to take a seat on the couch. Her ass barely grazed the mattress before she was fidgeting and rocking from side-to-side. I held my hand out to her, wiggling my fingers for extra measure. She rummaged through the silk robe she wore and pulled out $200. According to the lesson Vito gave me not too long ago, $250 could get her an eight ball. However, I was desperate for the cash and this wasn't my money, so I felt like I had nothing to lose by knocking the price down. I also knew I could make it work in my favor.

"You know, Sarah," I said as I returned with the eight ball hidden in one of my makeup bags, "Vito normally sells his product for more than this. BUT since he's out of town and left me in charge, I can lock this price in for you under one condition."

"Name it."

"You put me on to those buddies you told Vito you had looking to score. If you get me enough customers I can most definitely give you a decent discount."

Sarah accepted the bag gratefully. "Of course I can get you clients. My brother's a party promoter so he has access to clubs all over the city, not to mention he's throwing a bachelor party tonight. I can get you in. All you have to do is make sure you're dressed the part."

I took down Sarah's information, promising to give her a call later on. Staring at the two bills in my hand, I knew if I hustled hard that I could have this in the bag.

Literally.

✶✶✶✶✶✶

"Don't worry about a damn thing, Cash—you got this," I said to myself as I preened myself in the mirror one more time before I got ready to head upstairs to the hotel suite where my future customers were waiting. I had my hand on the door handle when my phone started buzzing in my purse. I bit my lip, contemplating on whether or not to answer, but made my decision once I raised it and saw Savion's name across the screen.

"Hey," I greeted him, as I settled back into my seat. "Or should I say 'Wah Gwaan?' How was the rest of the trip? Did you find out who popped off?"

Savion groaned in frustration. "Hell nah we ain't catch them niggas. Onyx had the entire island on lock down checking to see who got on airplanes at the end of the night, and came up with nothing. However, only a few of our most trusted employees knew about this trip, so Quade is in the middle of doing the process of elimination right now."

"You mean where he eliminates everyone? Savion, your brother is crazy as fuck," I joked. "I don't know how y'all handle him."

"Nobody handles Quade. The only person who's civilized him the least bit is ya girl. For the first time in his life baby boy took the initiative to not only plan dinner for them, but he also put on something other than some sweats. Shit, next thing we know, he might even start looking at a life outside of the game," Savion said wistfully.

"Do you ever think about life outside of the game?"

"Every once in a while"—I felt my heart lift—"then I think of how

124

much I enjoy my life the way it is and I change my mind."

"Oh," I replied casually, although I was kind of hurt by the idea that I wasn't included in his future. "I can't say I'm the least bit surprised, especially with the way you get around."

Savion laughed at the clap back but I could tell he didn't find anything remotely funny about it. "Someone sounds mad, too damn if you ask me because last I checked, you got a nigga."

"That's beside the point. When we were in Jamaica you said we were serious—"

"Because you wanted to tag along."

"Tag along? Now I'm a little fucking kid?"

"No, you're confusing the fuck outta me right now, Cash. One minute everything is good, and the next you're having a fit about not being included in my future when I know I'm not a part of yours."

"Because I'm finding it crazy that you've done everything to make me think we were actually moving in the right—you know what? I don't have time for this right now. I got business to handle," I said, hanging up on Savion.

I sat stewing in my anger for another five minutes. *This nigga ain't even bother to call me back to make sure I was okay,* I thought as I stomped through the hotel parking lot. I stared at my phone, hoping it would ring or maybe a text message would pop up. Nothing.

"Niggas ain't shit," I muttered, stepping onto the elevator.

I was alone on the ride up, which was exactly what I needed to get my mind right. I checked myself out in the mirror, admiring the black wrap dress I wore with my lucky Gucci sandals. They were on my feet during a shootout, a few fights, and held up through some long nights of partying. Plus, they went perfect with the oversized clutch I wore. Inside was packed to capacity with coke available in multiple gram sizes. My heart was beating in my throat with each passing floor. Tonight was the first night of my life where I went from kept to playing for keeps. I remembered as much as I knocked on the suite door. Seconds later a middle-aged white guy answered with a smile on his face.

"Hey," he said over the din. "You must be Sarah's friend. I'm Dillon."

One foot inside of the suite transported me to a scene straight out of a movie. There were strippers of all varieties entertaining the twenty men in attendance. Some were giving out lap dances while the rest of the girls performed with each other, kissing and grinding to the sultry beat coming from the Bose speakers dotting the spacious living room. A few heads turned in my direction, with some of them looking as if I was overdressed for the occasion, but one head nudge from Dillon changed all of that. I followed him to the back room, away from the noise and partying.

"What do you have on you?" he asked, closing the door behind me.

"I've got half grams, grams, and eight balls," I said, leaning against the desk behind me.

He rummaged through his pocket and came up with a wad of cash. I watched as he peeled off five crisp hundred-dollar bills. "I'll take two eight balls. One's for the bachelor. He's going to need it to get through his honeymoon; his wife's a complete bitch."

The transaction was as smooth as ever, with my pocketing my profit in record speed. There was a knock at the door, and next thing I knew, my clients were appearing in two's. I sold out of eight balls, grams, and only had a few half grams when I was finished selling.

"This is some of the purest shit I've had in a long time," Dillon said, watching me as I packed up. "Definitely up there with fish scale. You think I could get your number? I know plenty of people who would love to get their hands on this."

I exchanged numbers with Dillon, and like that, I had a repeat customer. Or should I say repeats. I was greeted with several business cards from stockbrokers, musicians, doctors, and lawyers, each one of them promising to get my number from Dillon so they could keep in contact with me. *I guess I was right for buying this burner phone,* I thought to myself with a self-satisfied grin as I left the hotel suite. It dropped the moment I caught a woman right in front of the elevator. She was dressed casually in a pair of jeans with a leather jacket and some Vans. No shade, but there was no way she would have any business on this floor, not dressed like she was at least. Or so I thought.

"What the fuck did you expect me to do, Steez? Punch the nigga in his face and force him to do business with me?" I felt my heart leap into my throat. "I asked him what the problem was. He said there wasn't one, but he had someone new…Yeah, we can hit up the club tonight and unload this shit real quick."

I watched her through the mirror, wondering how such a pretty girl could have a vulgar mouth. Her hair was the perfect shade of caramel with a pug nose and full lips currently curled up in anger. Our eyes locked for a split second through the reflection of the elevator with the doors springing open. I stepped off the elevator as quickly as I could, strutting to my car at top speed. I could hear her behind me, her sneakers making two slapping noises for every four I made. I reached into my cleavage for the little canister of pepper spray I kept there just in case I had to spray a bitch and run.

"I know you stole my fucking clients from me," she said, her voice bouncing throughout the deserted parking lot.

I shot her a glance over my shoulder. "I don't know what you're talking about, but what I do know is that you need to stop following me."

"I'll follow you for however long I feel like it, and I'll takes what's rightfully mine if I wanted to."

I turned around at the mention of her trying to rob me, and began to walk backwards towards my car, which I could see in the distance. "I don't have a motherfucking thing that belongs to you, and if you think you're going to put your hands on me without losing your life, you got another thing coming."

"You really think a prissy bitch like you can put fear in someone's heart?"

I jumped at the bark of laughter escaping her like a cough. Not wanting to play this game with this silly little girl any longer, I turned back around, high tailing it to my car. I pressed the unlock key and barely cleared my trunk when I heard her pick up her pace. I turned halfway around to hit her with my pepper spray when I felt the barrel of a gun pressed into my back.

"Where's all that mouth now, bitch?" she whispered in my ear. "Hmmm? I don't see it coming to your rescue and neither will that little canister of pepper spray from the check cashing place. You can't move weight and have the nerve to be carrying some fucking pepper spray. All it'll get you is your brains sprayed across the pavement."

"And it won't get you shit but put on every television screen in the city. I just came out of Dillon's hotel room. You don't think he'll put two and two together?"

"Him and all them white boys up there wouldn't risk their well being for no black bitches like us. Try again."

I took a deep breath, and said through gritted teeth, "Even if those white men up there don't give a fuck about me and don't say anything to the police, they'll know you did it, which means they still won't want anything to do with you. Judging by the way you're dressed you don't know shit about discretion. So go ahead, kill me, but you still won't get your customers back."

"You know what? Keep them niggas up there. I don't need them," she replied, removing the gun from my back. "But if I catch you in any of the clubs downtown, you'll have a whole new person to answer to."

I turned in time to see her disappear around the Hummer parked next to my car. Thinking this little bitch could change her mind at any moment, I hopped into my car and peeled off. Vito always described the game as being ruthless, with niggas willing to do whatever they had to in order to stay on top, but I had no idea shit could get real on my first day. I was starting to wonder whether or not it was worth it.

My decision was only made at the sight of the money pouring from my purse onto the living room sofa. I counted every single last dollar and including the cash I made from Sarah earlier, I had more than enough to pay my landlord. The market was wide open for me, and the money was there.

All I had to do was take it.

Quade

$\mathcal{I}$ sat watching her sleep, admiring her beauty. Her cinnamon skin could've easily been made of glass with the way it shined underneath the dim lamp lighting. She rubbed her small eyes with small, bejeweled fingers, pausing for a split second when she caught sight of me through her lids. Her rubbing became more fervent as she tried to figure out if her eyes were playing a trick on her. They popped wide open at the realization that I wasn't a mirage. She bolted upright, pressing herself into the quilted headboard of her king-sized bed.

"Who the fuck are you and how did you get in here?" she barked breathlessly, her chest heaving and pressing her breasts against the gold silk slip she wore.

I picked up the gun on my lap and stroked my chin with it. "I came here to talk to you about your man, Kenny. I know that nigga had something to do with my employee being robbed for ten bricks last week. Big Boy and Jerry said he was leader of the scheme. All I wanna know is where the rest of my shit is, and I think you can tell me that."

"Me? Listen, Kenny keeps me out of his business dealings. He said it's to protect me just in case I get hauled in by the police," she explained with a smirk on her face. "So as far as I'm concerned, you came in here and showed your face for nothing."

I chuckled at her snotty ass. "You a real bad bitch, Amaya. When

I heard that you were dating Kenny I was curious as to why when a beautiful woman like you could have any nigga that you want."

"I don't want any nigga; I want Kenny. We've known each other since we were kids, and after dating plenty of fuck boys, I realized the love of my life has always been right in front of me. He's always taken care of me, and if you think I'm getting ready to sell my man out, you thought wrong."

I leapt onto the bed and right into her lap, eliciting a yelp from her. Shorty started shaking so hard she was vibrating. She pressed herself into the headboard, trying to place as much space between us as possible. I almost felt bad for her except I remembered that I was here on business so nothing was personal. Using the barrel of my gun, I lifted her head until our eyes locked.

"Are you willing to die for Kenny?" She shook her head. "I ain't think so. Now I'm going to ask you a few questions and I need you to answer them as honestly as possible. Can you do that?"

Nod.

"Has Kenny been hanging around any new niggas?"

"No, he hasn't."

I pressed my gun deeper into her chin. "Don't sit here and fucking lie to me, Amaya. If I even get a hint of you lying I'll make you into some new room decorations, understand? My Glock been itching to end a bitch."

"About a week ago Kenny came in with cash—a lot of it. I asked him where he got it from and he told me it was none of my business. Later that night he got a call from someone asking him if he wanted to put some more work in. He agreed and they made plans to talk in the morning."

"Where is Kenny now?"

Amaya shrugged. "He left on Friday and promised to be back today."

"Where's your phone at?" I asked, searching the vicinity for her phone.

"I...I don't know," she replied, patting the sheets and pillows around her. A few pats later, she had her phone in her hand. "I've been calling him all day today. He hasn't answered."

"Try again. This time on FaceTime."

Amaya did as she was told. I slid the barrel of my gun exactly where her heart was located, giving her an incentive to play along. Kenny picked up on the third ring.

"Good morning, gorgeous," Kenny greeted casually. "I'll be on my way home in a few. I'm just tying up some loose ends for the week. I missed you."

"I missed you too. The house is so quiet without you." I mouthed a question to her, which she asked aloud. "So...how was your weekend? You looking a little sun kissed. I hope you didn't take any hoes on a vacation."

Kenny laughed. "I would never do you like that, Amaya. I was somewhere nice, but trust me when I say it was strictly business. These new niggas I'm working with are nothing but professional."

"You're working with someone new? I thought you, Jerry, and the rest of your boys were working as a team?"

"Babe, my niggas are gone, save for J Reed, and that's because he left town after he got those little crumbs I gave him. They were killed by that lil' Townsend nigga. My new team though? They're working on something for him. We would've had him handled if not for some unforeseen consequences."

"Kenny…please don't get wrapped up in the middle of something that has nothing to do with us," Amaya begged. "I know you have dreams of making some real money to get us out the hood, but I don't want you risking your life to do so."

"Amaya, there ain't no need to worry about any of that. You're only worried because you have no idea what these niggas are capable of…"

Tired of being quiet, I crept into the frame wit' a smile on my face. "I bet they're not capable of something like this."

Amaya broke down into tears. "Baby, please tell him whatever he wants. If you don't he's going to kill me."

"Who the fuck put you up to robbing me?" I barked, shoving my gun into Amaya's pretty face and using it to wipe her tears. "And don't lie, motherfucker, because you know I'll kill this bitch."

"Get that fucking gun outta my girl's face," Kenny said, panicking at the sight.

"Tell me what I need to know or else she won't have one in a few more seconds."

"Aight, I'll tell you. Just leave her alone."

"The faster you talk the faster I get this gun outta her face. Speak up, nigga!"

"Kenny, baby, please just tell him," Amaya cried. "Tell him who it was that came to our house a month ago."

A month ago? This bitch had been holding out on me and she was getting ready to lose her life off of that alone. I grabbed the back of her neck with my other hand, shoved the gun into her mouth, and shouted, "Speak MOTHERFUCKER!"

There was a slight motion behind Kenny's back. I saw it before he did, but before the words could leave my lips it was too late. A blade slid across his throat, sending rivulets of blood pouring down the front of the white tee he wore. The phone dropped from his hand, hitting the floor with a clatter and only providing a brief glimpse of the hooded figure holding Kenny up before tossing him aside. They crouched low, their hoodie obscuring their face in the shadows.

"You'll find out who the fuck I am when I'm ready for you to know. By then my .9 will be doing all the talking," he barked into the camera. He rose up slowly, and with one stomp of his boots, the phone broke, ending the call.

There was that shaking again. I glanced to my left to see Amaya holding back her sobs with a hand placed over her mouth. Common sense told me to kill the bitch too so she could meet up with her nigga in the afterlife, but I knew she was more valuable alive than dead. So, for the second time in the span of one week, I decided to let another witness live.

"Pack a bag so we can get out of here," I said, climbing off of her and returning to my seat next to the bed. "We ain't got all day either; someone is on their way to this apartment to handle you."

Amaya bristled at my words. "Get out of here? With you? Thanks to you my boyfriend is dead! I'm not going anywhere with you! I'll take my chances with whoever comes here, if someone even comes here."

"If they heard you mention a meeting from a month ago they'll be here soon to make sure you don't spill anything else." I rose from my seat. "But if you think you can handle those ruthless motherfuckers by yourself—"

"Give me fifteen minutes," Amaya huffed, climbing out of the bed and making a mad dash for her closet.

"I'll give you five."

Ten minutes later we were on the Williamsburg Bridge heading for the FDR Drive. If there was one place I could think of that Amaya would be safe, it was Zeus' place. Being the oldest and head of the operation, Zeus had a brownstone in the heart of Harlem with enough security to rival the Obamas. This nigga even put a couple cops on payroll to have them patrol his block more frequently than usual. Niggas would have to be a special kind of stupid to even think about becoming another statistic. I passed the first set of security on his block, two Lincoln Continentals like the ones used by detectives. As I pulled up out front I could see a fake cablevision van parked and a Cadillac Escalade parked on opposite sides of the street. This meant Zeus was home earlier than usual.

"This is your place?" Amaya asked, looking at my Champion sweats and hoodie with her nose turned up. "I would've never guessed."

"Well you guessed wrong. This is my brother's spot," I replied, shoving her towards the stairs. "The fuck I look like staying in something this nice."

Zeus was sitting in the living room watching the news when we entered. As usual he was dressed to the nines in a charcoal gray suit with a crisp white shirt and navy blue accessories. His eyes widened at the sight of Amaya standing there shifting her Louis Vuitton duffle bag in her hand.

"Who the fuck is this?" he asked, rising from his seat. "You bringing strays to my house now, Quade?"

"Have a seat," I ordered Amaya, who surprised me by obeying me with no questions asked. I beckoned for Zeus to follow me into his den. I closed the doors and said, "I was trying to extort some information out of Kenny by using his girl when someone killed him on FaceTime. I couldn't just leave her behind knowing she might have more information than she's letting on."

"That still doesn't explain why she's at the place where I lay my head," Zeus replied, pouring two tumblers of scotch from a cart parked in front of his wall of books. He handed me one and took a sip from the other. "We've got trap houses and warehouses for keeping people. Why didn't you take her to one of those places?"

"The first reason is because you have more than enough security to keep her safe. Niggas ain't brave enough to come up here and risk getting murked by the cops or even worse—arrested with some drugs planted on them."

Zeus shrugged in agreement. "True. What's your other reason?"

"I figured you could use a fuck toy and leave my girl alone," I smiled, taking a pointed sip of scotch.

"What are you talking about?"

"You didn't think I would hear about you tryna come on to Yara? Huh? Carrying her bags and smiling at her? She don't need nobody smiling at her but me," I said, pacing the room to keep my emotions under control. "So all that 'she bad as fuck lemme carry her bags' friendly shit you was tryna flatter her with? Dead that shit."

Zeus made a noise somewhere between a scoff and a laugh. "Are you getting territorial over this girl, Quade? Does she even know she's your 'girl'?"

"That doesn't concern you," I said, which was better than me admitting that I hadn't seen or spoken to Yara since Jamaica, so she was currently roaming around unaware that she was taken. "What does concern you is being my brother, and after seeing that I'm involved with someone, you shouldn't use that as an opportunity to fuck them."

The humor disappeared from Zeus' eyes. He was staring at me like he was itching to say something else, but settled with, "You're right. Yara's nothing more than a little sister from here on out. I shouldn't have even approached her like that. So...what's your plan for the girl?"

"I already told you: I get my information and you get some ass. But I think the only way I'll get all the information is if you get your ass first."

"You want me to fuck some random so we can find out who stole our shit?"

I nodded vehemently, glad that he was keeping up. "That's exactly what I want you to do. Her man is dead, she's feeling really vulnerable, and I'm sure she needs a place to live for the time being. You know how to play this, Zeus. Take one for the team."

"Are you sure she won't just give up the information?"

"She'll give up way more with sugar than with salt," I replied, tipping my tumbler back and downing the scotch.

Zeus' eyes widened in shock. "Quade, you're not supposed to—"

"Damn, that shit is strong," I said, pressing the tumbler into his chest and turning to leave. "Call me when you got some information. I gotta go off the grid for a few hours and handle some business."

Amaya was being served tea by Zeus' maid, Emma, a sweet older woman that was the closest thing any of us had to a grandmother. I inclined my head at her and received a wave in return on my way out the door. The block was still dead, which was a good thing because I was a little worried about being followed out here. With that not being the case, I figured it was time to put business to the side and finally catch up with my girl.

******

I stood by the receptionist desk of the Sweat Spot watching Yara and some cornball ass nigga chat. She was looking extra good in the mauve leggings she wore with a matching crewneck sweatshirt. On her feet were some well-worn Adidas, which showed me she spent a fair amount of time working out. There was nothing sexier than a woman that worked for what she wanted instead of taking shortcuts like these build-a-body bitches. To be quite honest, there wasn't a damn thing I would change about her body; she curved in all the right places, with my favorite part being her lips. A smile from Yara could make a cold nigga like me warm for even a brief second. It also had the ability to give hope in places you could never find.

Like in this nigga's mind while he flirted with my woman.

"My man, is there anything else you need help with?" I asked as I strolled up to the pair.

"Excuse me?" he said, crossing his arms to show off his muscle definition. "I'm in the middle of a gym tour."

"Quade, what are you doing here?" Yara hissed.

I ignored her completely, taking a step closer to her potential "client." "Your tour ended five minutes ago when you ended up in front of the same machines you started at. You can let the front desk know your decision," I said, mimicking his stance. "My nigga, you need me to sign it out for you?" I threw up my middle fingers, crossed them with each other twice, and pointed them towards the front desk.

"You know what? Yara, thank you for the tour. I'll be sure to give your name at the counter when I register," he replied slowly stalking past me like he was blessing me by not throwing hands, when in fact, he was lucky this was Yara's job and not the corner.

Yara tugged me over to a secluded section of the gym and started whacking me with her clipboard. "Quade, what the fuck are you doing at my job and why are you starting shit?"

"So I'm supposed to stand there quietly while this nigga is eye fucking the shit outta you?"

"No, he wasn't, Quade!"

"His corneas had you bent over getting that shit from the back. I don't know what kind of simp ass niggas you used to, but I'm not letting nobody look at my girl like that in my presence."

Yara's eyes widened in disbelief. "Your girl? Quade, I haven't heard from you in the past week. No call, email, text, nothing, and you show up telling me that we're in a relationship? Are you out of your mind?"

"Not more than usual."

"Quade, I can't do this right now. I have plenty of work to get done and if my boss catches me talking to you while on the clock, I'm gonna get—"

"Yara, is everything okay here?"

A buff middle-aged white man dressed in shorts and a muscle tee approached us. If I had to take one educated guess, this was the boss Yara was so afraid of, but I couldn't figure out why; it wasn't like he could do any real damage in that tight ass outfit without tearing a seam. Yara was shitting bricks, so I covered for her the best way I could.

"Yara was giving me a brief history of the facility before beginning our tour," I said with a polite smile. "To be honest the tour is a formality; I'm already sold."

At the mention of another client, Yara's boss backed off with a, "I'll be around if you have any additional questions. Yara?"

"I'll see you in a few, Dave," she answered with a polite wave. She slapped me on the arm once he was gone. "Really, Quade? He's going to be looking for a sale from me."

"And when I get my tour I'll make sure he gets it," I replied, bobbing on my heels, smiling at the aggravated look on her face.

Yara rolled her eyes, but that didn't stop her from beckoning for me to follow her. I took my sweet time catching up so I could appreciate the view, which was short lived when Yara turned around and began walking backwards, motioning to machines while rattling off their specs.

"I don't give a fuck about none of these machines," I said, cutting her off in the middle of her spiel. "I wanna know why you feel like you ain't my woman."

"Because I'm not! All we did was go out on one date. How does that translate into an exclusive relationship?"

"Easy: because after taking you out on a date I decided that I want you to be mine, so now you are."

"I don't know how you court your hoes, but staking a claim to me without my permission isn't going to fly. If you want to be with me then you need to show me. Properly."

"And how the fuck am I supposed to do that?"

"If you really want me I'm sure you'll figure it out," she replied with a pivot and continued on with the tour.

Growing up, I was one of the few kids on the block with both parents in the household. I watched my father treat my mother like a queen, but I assumed it was because she gave him four sons to carry on the family name. They had been married for ten years before I came along, so all my young mind could comprehend was that a man treats his wife like a queen. It never occurred to me that I had to do the same with my woman. Growing up with brothers that tossed women aside when they got tired of them didn't help either.

"Did you enjoy the tour?" Yara asked as she brought me around to the front desk.

I spent the entire time staring between her lips, hips, and thick thighs, which were all a treat to me. "Yeah. Uh…put me down for the one year platinum membership."

"Really?" Yara perked up. "You know you don't have to sign up if you already have a gym home."

"No, I don't have one, but now I have a reason to see you every day."

Yara gently tapped herself on the face with the clipboard. "Of course you do. Well, let's get to your registration…Can I see your state ID?"

I handed her my state ID, with the address used being Hasani's, being that he paid my bills for me. Yara noticed the address was different from where I had brought her the night of the club, but she remained mum. She was halfway through the application when she answered her phone.

"Hello, Amir." I stilled at the mention of another nigga's name and leaned in a little closer to listen. "What do you mean I have to pick up my stuff now? You know I'm at work. Why don't you bring my box to the shop and I'll pick it up there?" she scoffed at whatever his reply was. "Amir, I need that box. Everything in it is important to me, and you're fucked up for holding on to it the way you are. I told you I'm tired of the apologies, Amir, and I'm not coming back so there's no point of you holding on to my—Amir? Amir?" she stared at her phone in disbelief. "This nigga hung up on me."

"What does he have that belongs to you?" I asked casually.

"An important box," Yara replied, running her shaking hands through her hair. I could tell she was trying her best to keep calm. "Anyway, let me finish up this registration and see if maybe I can get off a little early."

A thoughtful silence developed between the two of us, with Yara's stemming from how she was going to get her box and mine thinking of how I was going to get the box first. I prepaid her for the membership in cash, accepting the complimentary duffle bag, shirt, and water bottle that came with it. She wished me a good day and hurried off, probably to find her boss. I stole one final glance at her, taking in the worried expression on her face. I didn't like it, and made a promise to myself to make sure it never happened again.

******

Thanks to my near photographic memory, I was back at Yara's old apartment complex without having to ask for directions. My only issue was figuring out what apartment she lived in. It was short lived at an older woman watching me from a table labeled *Tenant Patrol*.

"Good evening, young man," she greeted with a wave of her hand towards the notebook in front of her. "Can you sign in please?"

I signed in with a fake name I used from time to time, Terrell Cook. "I'm here to visit my brother, Amir, but I forget his apartment number."

"Amir? He's such a sweet young man; his apartment number is 3F," she replied back with a smile.

"Thank you. Have a nice day."

The apartment complex was busy for a Friday afternoon. People were lounging in the courtyard linking all of the apartment buildings together. Children played on the aged jungle gym as their parents looked on. Overall, it was just another day on the block and there was no need for me to worry about anyone giving me a second glance. I cleared the first and second floors without catching the attention of passersby or the cameras on each landing. Such little trouble had me feeling like this pop up was ordained, even more so when the door to 3F opened and I was met face-to-face with the bitch Zeus had been fucking.

"Quade," Sharise said, her eyes widening in surprise. "What are you doing here?"

"I'm here to pick up a box for Yara," I explained, bobbing on my heels and watching with mild interest as shorty tried to find a valid explanation for what she was doing here.

"Are you sure? Because Amir just got off the phone with her, and she said she was coming over to grab it."

"I'm positive."

"Okay...come in."

Sharise opened the door wide enough for me to slip in without much trouble. To be honest I wasn't sure what to expect, but this place definitely benefitted from Yara's touch. From the blue and gray walls to the matching sofa, accent rugs, and white tables, I felt like I was looking at one of those bougie ass furniture magazines. Sharise asked me if I wanted to take a seat, which I declined. There was no way in hell

I would sit in another nigga's house, especially when I knew nothing about him. With one fleeting glance in my direction, Sharise headed to the bedroom straight ahead. The bedroom door closed behind her, but that didn't stop me from hearing the conversation happening on the other side of it.

"What the fuck do you mean Yara sent some nigga to get her stuff?" I heard a rough voice bark. The bedroom swung open and Amir came rushing out with Sharise in tow. He stopped short of the dining room table, greeting me with a brusque, "Who the fuck are you?"

"Yara's new man. Where the fuck is her box at?" I asked, looking around for any sign of this box that obviously meant a lot to Yara.

Amir crossed his arms. "I already spoke to my Yara, and she's coming to pick up the box. You can sit down and wait for her if you want, but she's the only person carrying this box out of the apartment."

I shook my head. "Nah, you're gonna give me that box within the next sixty seconds or else."

"Or else what?"

I took a good look at Amir. He stood at roughly 6'4", which was a couple inches taller than me, and had a muscular build that could easily be earned with enough trips to the gym. Yes, he had fifty pounds on me, most of which was muscle, but there was one thing he was missing that he would never have—my heart.

"If you wanna wait the full sixty seconds to find out you're more than welcome," I replied with a shrug of my shoulders.

Amir was feeling himself because he was in his house, but Sharise knew what was up. I could see that for every five seconds that passed of Amir and me staring at each other, she would move away from him ever so slightly. I glanced at my Apple Watch, delighted at the sixty second mark passing so quickly. No sooner than I lowered my wrist did I charge at Amir, tackling him and sending him crashing into the dining room table directly behind him. The legs of the table splintered under the pressure, sending us plummeting to the floor. Dishes flew into the air hitting the walls with a crash.

"Quade, please don't do anything crazy!" Sharise screamed as she backed up and dashed into the bedroom. She returned with the box in hand. "Here! Everything Yara asked for is inside of it!"

Or at least that's what I thought I heard over the sound of my fist repeatedly slamming into Amir's face as I pummeled him unconscious. Somewhere between hitting the table and floor, he bumped his head, slowing down his reactions. His attempt to hit me with a left hook was thwarted by my right hand bending his back and proceeding to pound his face in. He gained some strength out of nowhere, using his lower body to flip me over so he was on top. I brought my legs up, wrapped them around his neck and changed the dynamic once again by pinning him to on the floor. This was the perfect time to whip out my Beretta and show him exactly what I planned on doing to him.

"I asked you for the box nicely, and that's rare because I don't respect a single motherfucker enough to ask for anything. You wanted to know what would happen if I didn't get the box? Close your fucking eyes and get ready to be greeted by some dead relatives," I said, pressing my gun right underneath his chin.

I was poised to pull the trigger when the front door opened, and in walked Yara with a startled expression on her face. Her eyes traveled from me, to a bloody Amir, to Sharise's scary ass, and ended on me. "Quade…what are you doing here?"

"I came to pick up your box," I replied as I rose to my feet, making sure to keep my gun trained on Amir, who was barely breathing. "I asked politely for the box, and this nigga told me 'no.' Can you believe that?"

"I damn sure can since that's exactly what he said to me," Yara said with a chuckle. Her eyes rested on Sharise. "And lemme guess: he invited you over here to make me feel some type of way?"

Sharise looked nothing but apologetic as she replied, "Yara, I was over here trying to make sure he gave you the box—"

"Bitch, I don't need you doing a damn thing for me so save all that fake ass 'looking out for my girl' shit for another one of them fake ass friends you have. I'll be taking my box now," Yara said, holding her hands out for the box.

"I know this entire situation has been a mess, Yara, but do you think maybe we could talk for a—"

"Quade, I have my box now, and I'm ready to leave," Yara said loudly, cutting off Sharise's begging.

"What you want me to do with this nigga?"

Yara stared down at Amir long and hard before she replied, "I guess you can let him live because I'm sure he's learned that next time I ask for my stuff it's on my time, not his."

Amir groaned from the floor as he came to long enough to catch my gun still trained on him. I would respect Yara's wishes for today, but I was tired of pulling out my gun for nothing. I fired off three shots, one on either side of Amir's face and one directly above it, eliciting screams from Sharise.

I knelt down and placed the piping hot barrel on Amir's forehead, laughing as it singed his skin. "Let that be the last time you ever call Yara, you understand me?"

There was no need for me to wait for his answer. I rose up to my full height and followed Yara from the apartment. People were looking to see what the source of the commotion was as we made our way back to the car. We drifted into a companionable silence along the way, with our shoulders brushing every now and then. She glanced at me a few times, probably trying to figure out how to ask the question of the day. I liked watching those pretty eyes of hers stare up at me in wonder, which was the only reason why I didn't answer her. It wasn't until we arrived at her car did she finally speak up.

"I had been stressing over grabbing this box all day long. Amir has it in his head that I'm the reason why everything went to shit, and it would've killed me on the inside to have to take a verbal beating from him for the sake of getting this box," Yara said, posting up on the side of the car as I placed the box into the trunk.

"That, and you might've broken your back tryna get it to your car. What the fuck you got in there?" I asked, slamming the trunk lid shut.

Yara approached me with this sultry grin on her face. For a nigga that stayed vigilant, I somehow ended up pressed against the trunk. "I can show you better than I can tell you. The contents of that box are personal, but I think I can make an exception for my man."

"Oh, it's like that now?" I laughed.

"It doesn't take dinner and a date to let a woman know that you care about her. Protecting her from anyone that means her harm is enough."

I pulled her close, reasserting my dominance over her and our relationship, and pressed her lips against mine. We were in this together from here on out, and I would always make sure she was safe.

Yara

*F*or all the heartbreak I had been through, Quade came through at the perfect time to make everything better. Of course it was common sense to wait a while before stepping back into a relationship, but for some reason unbeknownst to me, Quade made me lose all of my common sense. The entire ride back to my room, my stomach churned at the anticipation of being under such close quarters with him, especially after our semi-close call in Jamaica. But I promised him a look into my memory box, and I would give him one. This box contained the last memories of my life before my mother passed away and every happy moment after. I couldn't imagine life without this box, and because of Quade, I wouldn't have to.

"A hotel?" Quade said, staring from the Marriott hotel to me. "What are you doing staying at a hotel? Your friend wouldn't let you stay with her?"

I didn't approve of what Cash was doing by a long shot, but that didn't mean I wouldn't keep her secret safe with me. We did lunch a couple times this week, and from the looks of her appearance, she was doing just fine. She even mentioned wanting to move out of her current apartment to somewhere more private where she didn't have to worry about the wrong person having her address. Of course she let me know that I was always welcomed back whenever I wanted, but I politely declined.

"She's offered, but I'd rather stay here because it'll motivate me to find a place faster. I've already placed an offer on a few, but with my credit, I don't know if I'll get any of them." I rummaged through my purse and whipped out one of the two card keys I was given. "Here we are. I mean…it's not bad for a temporary living space. Plus I don't have to worry about coming home to it being untidy…Quade, what's wrong?"

"Pack your stuff up. You're staying with me," Quade said, placing the box on a neighboring table and proceeding to open the drawers and toss my clothes onto the queen sized bed behind him.

"Have you lost your mind?"

"No, but I think you lost yours if you think I'mma let you stay here when I have more than enough space."

"I already told you that if I wanted to stay with someone I could stay with Cash. I'm not going anywhere with you because I don't need your help. I don't need anyone's help," I said, tucking my injured wrist behind my back to make my case stronger. "Now please put my stuff back in the drawers."

Quade ignored me and instead grabbed my suitcase from the closet. I watched with mild interest as he neatly packed away all of my belongings by rolling them up military style. *I wonder who taught him that,* I thought to myself, knowing there was no way in hell they would let Quade join the military based off of his personality alone. I asked as much in order to break the awkward silence.

"My pops was a Marine. Growing up we had to be space efficient, which meant utilizing every inch of space to the max," Quade replied mechanically as he continued packing in a brisk manner.

"Is he the one who taught you how to…" I made a slicing motion across my neck and stuck my tongue out.

Quade smiled, and out of his mouth came one of the most carefree laughs I had ever heard. In that split second I could see the side of him that might've prevailed if not for circumstance. He shook for a few more seconds and went back to packing with a residual smile on his face.

"Nah, I learned that after my moms passed. It was the only way I could deal with losing her," he explained, his smile dropping as he turned back into his usual self. He placed the rolling suitcase on its feet and said, "You ready?"

"I told you that I'm not going anywhere with you."

Quade picked up my memory box with his other free hand and made his way to the door. He lifted one foot and artfully opened the door by pressing down on the handle. "You can stay here if you want, but your stuff will be at my place."

"Fine," I huffed, grabbing my purses from the closet and following behind him. "I don't get why you have such a problem with me staying in a hotel though."

The elevator doors sprung open as I approached, half out of breath compared to a cool and calm Quade, who didn't even break a sweat considering all the stuff he was carrying.

"I'm only coming with you because my wrist is too fucked up for me to fight you over my stuff."

Quade scoffed. "If that's what you need to tell yourself."

I leapt off of the elevator the second the doors were wide enough for me to squeeze through. The front desk associate was kind enough, offering me a sympathetic smile as I explained to her that I was checking out earlier due to a family emergency. As I rummaged through my purse to pay the couple weeks that I stayed, all I heard Quade say was, "Here you go."

"You don't have to pay for my room," I said, holding out my card to the woman. "Here you go, Miss."

Quade shot the woman a look that said to ignore me, which she did, cashing him out and giving him his change. With my second battle lost, I knew it made no sense to keep arguing, but I wasn't going to simply submit to him either. I spent the entire ride to his apartment sulking as I stared out the window. Quade ignored my sullen mood to the point where I wondered if he remembered that I was there. My thoughts were answered when he pulled up at a supermarket and hopped out without a backwards glance. He reappeared at my door, opening it and helping me out like a gentleman.

"I ain't got shit at the crib but some chicken and maybe a few slices of pizza, but I remember you said you don't like eating outside food. I figured it would only be right to make a quick stop here so you could get some groceries," Quade explained as he grabbed a shopping cart and disappeared into the supermarket."

Being inside of the supermarket brought some normalcy into my life. I loved cooking, and missed it dearly when I moved into the hotel. Two weeks of eating restaurant food had my stomach feeling funny as fuck. I smiled at the thought of placing it all behind as I filled the cart with fruits, veggies, and lean protein, all of which Quade was giving the side eye.

"You don't have to eat any of what I plan to cook, but you should," I said while deciding whether I wanted Jasmine rice or quinoa. I ended up choosing both. "One week of clean eating with me will have you feeling like a new man. Your skin will start glowing, you'll have more energy, and you might even become a little more levelheaded."

"I'm very levelheaded, thank you very much," Quade replied as he dumped a bunch of sugary cereals into the cart. "I don't need an apple to help me decide whether or not I wanna kill someone."

I rolled my eyes at his dramatics. "The apple won't make that decision for you, but carrots will help with your eyesight so you don't miss, and one of my blueberry flaxseed smoothies will have you focused as fuck. Trust me on this; I know what I'm talking about."

From then on Quade didn't object, and even replaced a couple of his sugary cereals for some healthier ones. I was convinced that I might've gotten through to him until we pulled up at Popeyes on the way home.

"Deadass?" I asked incredulously.

Quade placed his order, which was just as large as it had been the last time we came through, and headed to the window. "What? I gotta have something else in case I don't like your bird food."

"How about this? I make dinner tonight and if you don't like it, I promise to never stand between you and your Popeyes ever again. Right hand to God."

Quade paid for his food and accepted the bag from the cashier. "Aight, let's see what you got, ma."

I spent the rest of the ride thinking of the perfect recipe to cook up for the picky eater Quade. Judging by his obvious choice of chicken all the time, he didn't like too many other meats. *Or maybe there was no one to make it for him,* I thought, knowing there was a good chance that after the death of his mother he didn't eat the best. I decided to play it safe tonight and opted to make oven-fried chicken with three cheese macaroni and cheese, yams, red beans and rice, and homemade biscuits. Once I stepped foot into Quade's compact kitchen I was back in my element as I began to prep dinner. Quade watched me out the corner of his eye as he put away the groceries.

"You got a radio? I like to listen to music while I'm cooking," I said to Quade, who took a seat at the kitchen counter and began watching me.

"Nah, I ain't got a…wait a minute, I might have something…"

Quade slid out of his seat and disappeared into the bedroom. He returned a few minutes later with a brand new Beats pill. I could tell it was a gift he never considered using, which made me wonder if he spent his time at home in silence. There wasn't a television in sight, so what did Quade do in his free time?

"Hasani bought this for me last Christmas. I got a closet full of weird shit my brothers like buying that I have no interest in."

"Such as…?"

"A couple TV's, PlayStation 4, Xbox One, a shitload of games, a sound bar…mad random shit." Quade matched my surprised face with his confused one. "What?"

"Nothing, I'm just surprised that you don't play any video games or do anything else that might be considered fun. Do you ever have fun? Like what was the last fun thing you ever did?"

Quade shrugged. "I don't know. Life ain't all about fun when there's business to be handled. I got a lot on my plate, and there's no room on it for fun."

"That's where you're wrong. Sometimes you have to forget about everything going on in your life and enjoy yourself. Like I'm getting ready to do once I put this chicken in the oven."

Quade reclaimed his seat and watched me prepare dinner. As promised, once I placed the breaded chicken breasts into the oven, I linked my phone to the pill and seconds later, the once silent house was filled with music. OutKast's "The Way You Move" had me dipping my hips and spinning to the beat. I sang along as I finished up my prepping. Pharell and Rihanna's new song came on, which was a twerk favorite, and I danced to that as well.

"You're crazy," Quade said over the music.

"Coming from you, I'll take that as a compliment," I said, changing the song to something a little slower.

Kendrick Lamar's "Loyalty" blasted through the speakers. I walked up on Quade rapping the lyrics, which earned me another one of those rare smiles. He wrapped his arms around me and rapped Kendrick's verse with ease. I followed up with Riri's verse, delivering it with the right amount of sex appeal so he knew it was real. Kendrick's bridge came on and although it was lighthearted, I could tell that

Quade really wanted to know if I was ready to be with him.

Tell me who you loyal to

Is it love for the streets when the lights get dark?

Is it unconditional when the 'Rari don't start?

Tell me when your loyalty is coming from the heart

I answered with a kiss, letting Quade know that no matter what came our way, I would always stand beside him. We met with no secrets between us and that would always stay the same.

******

"Damn that was good," Quade said, rubbing his stomach as he sat on the couch. "You got it, ma. I'll lay off the Popeyes—"

"And McDonalds, and Burger King, and Wendy's..."

"Wendy's food is fresh though."

I side eyed him from the kitchen, where I was packing everything away. "Mmmhmm...well I don't want another woman feeding you, whether she's real or not," I joked. "It's about time you started treating your body better. You only get one."

"That's the thing though. I don't care about what happens to my body because I don't plan on being here much longer. I live every day like it might be my last one."

I stopped packing and posted up against the counter. "If you don't plan on being here much longer then why make me your lady? I'm tired of losing people, Quade. If you're going to live your life like one long ass suicide mission then maybe we need to slow down."

"I thought you were one of the few people that understood my job and how my future isn't guaranteed."

"I do, I just don't like the idea of you going out of your way to make sure you die."

Quade rose from his seat with a lazy smile on his face though his brows were knitted with concern. He placed his hands on the counter and leaned in close enough for me to smell the chocolate cake on his breath from dessert.

"We all gotta go one day, Yara. I'm just more comfortable with the fact that I might be going sooner rather than later. It means that I appreciate life more than niggas that will do anything to elongate theirs. I don't wanna live longer if it means losing respect from the streets or my integrity, point blank period." He gently grabbed my chin between his finger and thumb, lifting my face to meet his. "Instead of worrying about the time I won't be here, focus on the time I am. Like right now. I can give you more attention in the span of four years than some niggas will ever be able to in a lifetime."

I didn't want to accept Quade's acceptance of a premature death, but I knew the best way I could show him that life was worth living was by showing him its beauty. Of course it would probably take some kicking and screaming on his behalf, however, I think he's worth it. Quade leaned in closer, planting a kiss on my lips. My cheeks heated up as the kiss intensified. I had been given a clean bill of health by my doctor, which gave me the green light to take things to the next level, but I was scared to let Quade know about my limits.

"How about I show you my memory box? That was the whole point of me inviting you back to my hotel room," I said, slipping out of his embrace and heading towards the bedroom.

Quade wrapped me up in his arms again, peppering kisses down my neck. "How about I focus on another box right now?"

"Or, you can come sit down with me and take a look at these pictures," I said, slipping out of his grip once again and dragging my memory box over to the bed. "Lift this up for me, please?"

Quade plopped down on the bed, placing the box between us. I pulled off the lid and was instantly brought back to my childhood. I picked up Nettie, the rag doll that my grandmother created for me before she passed away. I didn't remember much of her—I was four when she died—but this doll had gotten me through plenty of tough nights. I held it tight on the nights where my parents would argue and fight. It kept me sane when my father walked out on us and never looked back. Nettie was also the only one I could talk to about my mother's new boyfriend and how much I hated him. I opened my mouth to tell Quade these exact words and choked on them. I pressed Nettie into my chest and broke down in tears, thinking of how disappointed my mother would've been in me if she saw the way I allowed myself to be treated by Amir over the past few months. My legs locked into my chest, and I lay on my side with my back turned to Quade, who sat immobile. I felt the weight of the box disappear, replaced by Quade hovering over me.

"Um…you okay?"

"Of course I'm not okay," I snapped, burying my face into Nettie's chest.

Silence.

"You ain't the only one with a dead mother," Quade said after a minute.

I removed Nettie from my face and shot back, "I know, but I'm sure you didn't have to watch your mother die. I was there. I hid in the closet and held this doll as he choked her to death."

A hollow laugh escaped Quade's lips. "She said I didn't watch my mother die..." he muttered to himself. He plucked Nettie from my embrace and shouted, "Your mother was choked to death, which takes roughly five minutes to cause irreversible brain death. That's a fairly quick death. I had to watch my mother rot in a bed and become so weak she couldn't even wipe her own mouth let alone her own ass. My beautiful mother turned into a corpse right before my own eyes and there wasn't a damn thing I could do about it! She went from smelling like to Chanel to smelling like death. My brothers could barely stand the sight of her, but I took care of her the best I could. I caught a cold and there was this tickle in my nose. I hurried to the hallway and let it out, made sure to wash my hands before going back to her, but that wasn't enough. She was dead two days later. I fucking killed my mother with a sneeze, Yara. I've never told anyone that story, not even my brothers. Not that you would give a fuck because instead of seeing that I cared enough to ask, you shut me out."

Quade climbed off the bed and disappeared, slamming the bedroom door behind him. His words stung because they were true. I was so used to Amir being perfect in every way possible that I had become accustomed to being misunderstood. Now I pushed away the one person who could truly relate to what was going on.

******

I found him in the living room doing pushups. He was covered in a light sheen of sweat. *I guess this is what he does all day since he doesn't have a television,* I thought as I approached him. Not wanting to scare him, I dropped to my knees, crawled the rest of the distance, and sat cross-legged in front of him. He didn't miss a beat at my entrance, continuing to exercise as if I wasn't there. After the way I showed my ass I couldn't say I blamed him. Ten minutes later I knew this could take a while. I lay down beside him and crawled underneath him. He went into a plank, which gave me enough space to get everything off my chest.

"I'm sorry for acting like a brat. You were trying to be there for me and instead of being grateful, I acted like a bitch." I bit my lip. "The story about your mother—"

"Don't worry about it," Quade replied.

"What you told me was—"

"Like I said, don't worry about it."

Just when he had let his guard down a little, I had to fuck up and have it snap back up. Closing my eyes, I tried to think of some way, any way I could fix this.

"I have trust issues, Quade. Plus some regular issues too, like only being able to fuck in the missionary position because I watched my mother be violated by her boyfriend too many times to believe that pain is part of love. I'm scared of the dark because every time I turn off the lights I've lost part of myself or someone that I love. Sometimes both. I have spent so much of my life being misunderstood that when someone came along just as fucked up as me, I turned a bonding moment into 'whose the biggest victim?' not realizing that you'll win at it every time."

Quade dropped to a low plank. He studied me for a full minute before asking, "You only fuck in the missionary position?"

"Is that all you really took from my speech?"

"I heard the rest, I'm just stuck on trying to figure out what type of dick down you could possible get in the missionary position."

I rolled my eyes. "Why do I even bother…"

"Because you like me," Quade replied with a kiss. He raised his arm and moved my hair from my face. "Since you like me, you need to also remember that you can trust me. I can't be here for you if you shut yourself off to everyone, including me."

I wrapped my arms and legs around Quade, thinking I could make him topple to the floor. He remained firm, which was a pleasant surprise. If he could hold me down physically, then there was no way I could cut him off mentally. For once in my life I stopped being scary, playing it safe, coloring inside the lines Yara and opened my heart to Quade and the unlimited possibilities to come.

Cashmere

"Good afternoon, welcome to Lieberman, Schwartz, and Donahue, how may I help you?" the friendly receptionist said from her desk at one of the most prestigious law firms in the city.

I wiggled the box in my hand. "I'm here to deliver a package for Gary Mathers."

"Sure. Let me call ahead to make sure he's in his office," she replied, picking up her phone and making a quick call. A few nods later, she said with the receiver still to her ear, "Mr. Mathers is waiting. Just go straight down this hall and make a right at the corner. He's the first door on your right."

I followed her directions to a tee and ended up at a swanky corner office with a breathtaking view of the city. Gary was sitting behind his desk reading through a huge stack of papers, his eyes moving from side-to-side at a rapid speed. I knew that look after servicing a few white-collar cokeheads over the past two weeks. Once you start dealing to doctors, lawyers, stockbrokers, and other "prominent" members of the community, you start to notice how different they move. Today was no different; Gary was handsome, with a head full of jet black hair, perfect teeth, and a muscular body underneath his Armani suit, but once I took a good look at those cerulean eyes that were currently bloodshot from a lack of sleep, my thoughts immediately went to Vito. There was nothing remotely attractive about dating a cokehead, no matter what position they held.

"Cash," he said with a smile. "Close the door, come on in, have a seat."

I closed the door behind me and took a seat at the edge of his desk. I wasn't a client and had no need of his services, so there was no way in hell I planned on sitting my ass in one of his chairs, creating the assumption that we were equals. I needed to look down on him so he knew that he needed me. This was one of the many lessons I got from watching gangsta movies over the weekend. Without Vito, I had no clue how to assert myself in most of these situations, which left me to do what I thought was right. Like sitting at the edge of the desk tapping the box on my hand while Gary looked on expectantly.

"You know how this goes…"

"Oh yeah." Gary reached into his suit jacket and pulled out twelve crisp hundred-dollar bills. "Here you go…"

I handed him the box and slipped the cash into my bra. "Nice doing business with you."

I waved goodbye to the receptionist on my way out, making sure to be as friendly as possible because she would be seeing a lot more of me. If Gary liked my product then I was sure he would recommend me to more of his buddies, securing my bag for the rest of the year. I had already made almost a hundred grand over the past two weekends just hitting up events that were referred to me by Sarah and Dillon. With my supply down to its last half a kilo, I was worried about how I was going to re-up since I had no idea where Vito had gotten his product from in the first place. Soon I would have to get in contact with his brother, Wale, who was a small time hustler but still had connections nonetheless. My burner phone buzzed with a call from Dillon, giving me a moment of peace away from my worries.

"Hey, Dillon. What's up?" I asked in the privacy of my car.

"Are you busy tonight?"

How can I have a name like Cash and ever be too busy to make money? "No, I'm free tonight. Are you throwing another party?"

"Actually, a friend of mine is hosting at a club downtown and he wants someone to come through with some good shit. I told him about your stuff, gave him a taste, and he's already put the word out that you'll be there."

"Cool, what's the name of the club?"

"Sphinx. Your name's on the list. All you need to do is ask for Alex when you get there."

"Got it. Good looking out, Dillon. See you around."

I did a dance in my seat, brimming with joy at how successful I had been over the past two weeks. The money was coming in, I just moved into a new apartment, and I was finally doing something for myself. At the rate I was going, I would have enough money to be able to pull clothes for my styling business. So far, I managed to build an Instagram following of 20,000 just by doing some share for shares and buying promos from celebrities. I refused to be like Vito, who made the game a drug he couldn't quit. I planned on having something for myself by the end of the year.

******

I found Yara standing on the corner of a quiet street in the middle of Bed Stuy. She was dressed real cute—a black latex dress with a pair of strappy heels and her hair hanging around her face in deep waves—and there was a glow about her I had never seen before. She smiled brightly at me as she climbed into the passenger seat.

"Damn, bitch. You looking like money in this brand new convertible," Yara said, giving my Mercedes Benz a decent once over. It was candy apple red and kept my black one company.

"I figured with all of the hard work I've been putting in I might as well give myself a little upgrade," I replied, giving my shoulder a playful brush.

"You know, I'm not too fond of how you're getting money but as long as you stay safe, Cash, I'll support you no matter what. Just don't ask me to move no weight," Yara joked.

The tension I had been feeling since we got back from Jamaica disappeared at that moment. Yara and I had done lunch together a few times since my decision to move weight, but my new occupation always seemed to hang in the air. With Yara's approval, I felt more secure in what I was doing. I didn't need it, but with her being the only family I had, it was good to have. We turned up on the way to the club just like old times before ain't shit niggas and fake friends came into the mix. I was on a hundred when we entered Sphinx and wanted nothing more than a drink in one hand while I made money with the other.

"Where are you headed?" Yara asked as I slipped out of our VIP section. "We just got here."

"I need to see the promoter for the night. He was able to get me a section on such short notice so I wanna thank him real quick. Plus, I gotta get us something to sip on."

Alex was lounging around in a section of his own when I found him. The two model type bitches flanking him looked me up and down, trying real hard to find a flaw in the Gucci romper I wore with a pair of Giuseppe Cruel pumps. I flicked a handful of hair over my shoulder so they could get a better look at the bitch they obviously were pressed to be. Alex, a skinny Italian dude, appreciated the show, his eyes hungrily roaming up and down my body. He rose from his seat with one of his thin hands outstretched. I shook like the businesswoman I was and got right down to business.

"For tonight I've gotten the owner, who's a good friend of mine, to look the other way under the premise that you only sell to people I've selected. If their friends want anything they'll have to place an order with that person and so on. You got a system?"

I gave my purse an inconspicuous pat. "I sure do. How will I know who you selected?"

"They'll place their order with my bottle girl, Priscilla, and she'll leave a shot glass of mints on the table. White mints mean half grams and pink ones mean eight balls. You greet them with hugs and kisses, make the exchange and keep it moving. Capiche?"

Alex's system worked like a charm. After making sure Yara was good, I made my rounds, hugging each of the handsome guys that greeted me and giving air kisses to the women. They were buying grams out the ass, but the final table, with a fine ass Chris Pine lookalike sitting at the helm, purchased five eight balls and ten half grams between the ten of them.

"You're much prettier than the last girl that used to come buzzing around here," he said in a thick British accent. He held out a business card. "Nigel's the name. I might require your services again in a more… intimate setting."

I placed the business card in my pocket and replied with the wink of my eye, "I'll be sure to give you a call."

Yara was shaking her ass in the VIP section when I returned. Her newly healed wrist was helping her hand make imaginary money rain to Yo Gotti's "Rake It Up." Now that I was done working, I could kick back and have some fun with my girl. We popped a few more bottles, compliments of Alex, ate some delicious boneless buffalo wings, and were completely fucked up as we staggered from the club. We were halfway to the car when I heard someone say, "Didn't I tell you not to come onto my territory or I would lay you flat, bitch?"

I turned in time to feel a fist connect with my cheek, snapping my neck around. The force of the blow knocked me into my car. Yara reacted faster than I did, kicking her heels off and charging at the girl who hit me. Homegirl wasn't expecting so much strength from a drunk and got knocked to the ground by Yara. I rummaged through my purse, looking for my pepper spray.

"Who's laid flat now, bitch?" Yara roared, holding her by the hair with one hand and pummeling her with the other. "Huh? Huh? Throw some fucking hands, hoe."

I had my spray poised to shoot when a gun was placed to Yara's forehead. Somewhere in the midst of the fight two men had approached us. They were giants, each towering over us and staring down with cold, hard eyes. Yara let go of the girl, but not without shoving her head into the cement sidewalk. My girl was real bold right now, and I was scared that she was gonna fuck around and end up with a hole in her head.

"Get up off of her before I spray you all over this concrete, lil' bitch," the gunman said, giving Yara a hard shove in the head with the barrel of his gun. "Lauren, you good?"

"I'm good, but I see the bouncer down the street coming this way. Let's get out of here," Lauren said once she was on her feet.

The other giant gave her a hard shove. "We ain't going no fucking where until you handle this bitch for putting her fucking hands on you. And what about this one? Didn't you say you told this bitch to stay off of our territory?" He held the gun out to her. "Murk the bitch. Steez is down the block waiting."

"You ain't putting a hand on either one of us unless you want some fucking problems," Yara spat, her nostrils flaring. "We were invited here to have a good fucking time and we did. Right, Cash? Cash?"

I was too busy having a stare off with Lauren that I forgot where I was and what was going on. "Listen, I just sold off the last of my work so you ain't gotta worry about me anymore, okay? I'm fucking done with this shit and you can have your fucking club back."

"That ain't good enough"—the gunman placed his gun underneath my chin, digging into my throat to the point where I couldn't breathe—"we gave you a warning before, bitch, and you ain't listen. So now you gotta pay the consequences, you and your little Chihuahua of a friend."

"Leave my girl outta this; she ain't do nothing. Whatever beef you got is with me," I said, trying to keep my eyes from crossing and the liquor rumbling around in my stomach from erupting out of my mouth. "You want money? I got money on me. Take it and leave her alone."

"Bitch, you think we give a fuck about your money? That ain't what this is about. This is about you selling on our territory after we gave you a pass one time." The barrel traveled from my throat to my lips. "You got any last words?"

"Let her go!" Yara screamed. There was a scuffle and she shouted, "Get off of me. Let me go!"

I laid my head back against my window and closed my eyes, feeling the world spin around me as I readied myself to make my ascent to heaven. The moment never came because I heard someone yell, "What the fuck is your dumb ass doing holding someone up in the middle of Manhattan?"

"Steez—"

"And you saying my name out here, too?"

The gun disappeared from my forehead as the gunman plead his case. "I ain't mean to—"

"You ain't mean to do a lot of shit. If you gon' pop on a nigga then pop. Like I am right now."

Shots popped off, two of which hit the gunman in the head and neck. He dropped to the floor with a thud, his head hitting the sidewalk with a resounding thud. His partner was next, shaking as he was lit up with bullets. Yara dropped to the floor without a second of hesitation

171

while Lauren stood there biting her lip.

"Get in the fucking car, man!" the voice shouted to her.

Lauren shot me a fleeting look before running out into the street. I turned in time to see a black Yukon Denali peel off down the street, leaving the two of us in shock. I fumbled through my purse until I found my keys, crying the entire time. Yara grabbed her purse and shoes from the floor, cussing under her breath as she stumbled into the backseat. I sped off right behind the Yukon, praying to God that no one caught my plates and hauled us in behind someone else's bullshit.

"Cash, what the fuck happened back there!" Yara barked. "You're supposed to be a fucking drug dealer and when a bitch rolls up on you you're too fucked up to fight back? You were ready to let that nigga kill you instead of coming back with some heat of your own! You mean to tell me that you blew all this money on a new whip and you didn't even consider getting a fucking gun to protect it with? Or better yet, to protect yourself with?"

"Yara, not right now," I groaned as I tried to remember how to get back to my place without taking any main streets. "I feel bad enough as it is."

"As you should. What if their boss didn't pull up? We'd both be two dead bitches. How can you be so stupid, Cash?"

"BECAUSE I'M NOT YOU YARA!" I roared at the top of my lungs. "I've been doing this for like five fucking minutes! I know I should've been got a gun, but I haven't had the chance to find an arms connect. Trust me, after tonight, my first move is to get my hands on a piece if it's the last thing I do."

"It should've been done from the very beginning. You know, when you decided to get into illegal activities. I shouldn't have to leave out of the club all fucked up to then start fucking a bitch up while you freeze up! If you're gonna be scared to handle niggas then maybe you need to pick another vocation."

I stopped at a red light and banged my head against the steering wheel. "Yara, can you please shut the fuck up for like five minutes? You think I don't feel bad about what happened?" I cried. "I have been scared every single night I leave out to handle business that it might be my last. What if I'm pulled over by the cops one night? What if a customer flips on me? What if I get robbed? I froze up because I was scared, but trust, I won't pull some dumb shit like that again. I'mma run this motherfucking town if it's the last thing I do. I'mma have some goons, soldiers, and more than enough money to make sure we ain't ever gotta go through something like this ever again, you hear me?"

Snore.

"Yara?"

Snore.

I turned back and there was Yara slumbering peacefully, her shoes moving up and down on her chest. She was out for the count and I already knew it was gonna be hell getting her into my apartment. A car honked from behind me, shaking me out of my daydream. I entered the game thinking I would be able to maintain my lifestyle, hold Vito down while he was in rehab, and save for my styling business with little to no trouble. It was naïve of me to believe that my first run in with homegirl would be my last. She brought goons to a gunfight while I brought fear.

173

Nope, there was no way in hell I would ever be that stupid again. The next time I ran into Lauren I would draw on her ass so she would know I was not only about my business, but I was also officially about that life.

******

Yara's diatribe rang through my mind all night. Although she apologized in the morning, blaming the shock of the situation for her anger, I still felt like it was a well-deserved cussing. I was never one to go groveling to someone for some help, but I knew there was no way I could go another day without an adequate amount of protection, which was exactly how I ended up on Savion's doorstep. He answered on the second ring with a tumbler of Henny in his hand. I was saved from an awkward introduction by someone yelling in the background for him to hurry up and get back to the game.

"Don't run now, nigga!" Hasani said clearly, despite the blunt dangling from his lips. "Come back and get this—oh shit. Wassup, Cash?"

"Hey, Hasani," I said with a polite wave to him and his girl, Gia, who sat quietly by his side, watching the game with mild interest.

After Quade and Yara, Gia and Hasani had to be one of the oddest pairings I had ever seen. Don't get me wrong; Hasani was fine. He had rich mahogany skin with delicate features, a slim nose, and sensual lips that resembled melting pieces of chocolate each time he licked them. But Gia, with her coffee and cream skin, hazel cat eyes, thick curly hair, and soft voice, seemed like she would rather hang around the library than the Townsend Brothers. A book was currently sitting on her lap,

174

His Savage was Her Weakness by Tya Marie. The sultry cover had me thinking maybe Gia had a thing for thugs, like me.

Savion gave his tumbler a twist. "Thirsty?"

"I could drink."

I followed him down the hall of his loft house, admiring how beautiful it was. The walls were filled with classic Brooklyn prints, like Junior's, the Brooklyn Bridge, Myrtle Promenade, and Prospect Park. His kitchen was spotless: pots and pans hung up above the kitchen island, spices lined the spice rack, and I could see tons of packaged food in the glass cabinets along with real plates. *Who would've thought the Townsend Brothers had so much class?* I thought as I took a seat at the kitchen island.

Savion rummaged through the stainless steel refrigerator as I continued studying my surroundings. He emerged with a bottle of Ciroc, cranberry juice, and a carafe of orange juice. My brows furrowed at the colander, thinking, *there's been a woman in his life at some point in time; niggas know nothing about carafes.*

"Vodka cool?" he asked, rummaging through the cabinets until he surfaced with a glass.

"Sure."

Savion proceeded to whip me up a perfect passion sunrise. His measurements were meticulous, and one taste had me impressed. "Damn, you went to bartending school or something?"

"Nah, when I was younger I used to mix drinks for my parents whenever they had parties," Savion explained, taking a sip of his drink. "When we were all younger, my parents made us all have a legit hustle in the event that the streets got too hot for us to handle business. Hasani's an accountant, Zeus is a mechanic, I'm a bartender—"

"And Quade?"

Savion snorted into his drink. "Photography."

"Quade a photographer? I can't see it..."

"Those are his prints on the walls."

I pointed to the wall. "Quade? 'Trigger-happy, will shoot you between the eyes, doesn't take shit from anyone' Quade? Wait until I tell Yara..."

"Him and Yara are together?" Savion silently chuckled. "So that's why this nigga had me out furniture shopping all day yesterday. Damn, he's got it bad for your girl. She's got a surprise coming to her when she gets home. So...what you called me for? To apologize for showing your ass two weeks ago?"

"Savion..."

"Bruh, I'm too grown to be playing games. You got a whole nigga at home and you think I'm gon' rearrange my entire life for you? Nah..."

"I wasn't looking for you to rearrange anything. All I wanted to know was that you have the ability to think ahead."

"Of course I have it—for someone that's not into playing games. You still got a man, don't you?"

I closed my eyes and rolled them so hard they almost got stuck in back of my head. "It's complicated."

"Which is another way of saying when shit is complicated you gon' try to slide this way. Fuck outta here with all that mess. What did you really call me for?"

"I need a gun. Or two."

Savion's grimace disappeared, immediately replaced by shock and concern. "What do you need a gun for?"

"For protection."

"Ya nigga can't get you a gun?"

I sucked my teeth. "If I could get a gun from my man, trust me I would. But I know you can get me something without any bodies on it." I downed the rest of my drink, grateful for the buzz that followed shortly after. "Please, Savion."

"Aight, give me a minute."

I grabbed the bottle of Ciroc sitting on the counter and poured myself shots, each one hitting better than the next. I figured since it was my last time drinking I might as well make it count. My entire mouth was numb from my fourth shot when Savion appeared with Hasani and Gia, who was carrying a briefcase. My cheeks burned with embarrassment; I didn't want everyone to know that I was having trouble protecting myself.

"I don't know whether or not you noticed, but Gia stayed behind while we were in Jamaica because she's our official arms dealer," Hasani said, taking the briefcase from Gia and placing it gently onto the kitchen table.

"My mother's side of the family has some ties to the mob," Gia explained as she fingered the pistols inside of the briefcase. "My family deals in arms, mostly importing and exporting throughout the East

Coast."

"But when she isn't dealing guns she's going to school to become a doctor," Hasani finished, momentarily dimming the bright smile on Gia's face.

Gia nodded in agreement, but I could tell she wasn't too into it. "Yes, I am a pre-med undergrad at Columbia by day, and one of the most well-known arms dealers in New York by night. So, what are you looking for?"

"I'm looking for something not too big, but big enough to do some damage if it needs too. A gun that when I pull it out niggas know I mean business, but also cute enough to go with whatever I'm wearing."

Gia waved her hands over the guns, thinking on which would be perfect and settled on a Kimber Pro Carry II. "This one is perfect. I have it as a .45 and a 9. It has a grip safety, which reduces the chances of an accidental discharge. It's not too heavy, the magazine capacity is 7+1, and this steel goes with anything. Here, hold it and see how it feels."

I accepted the gun from Gia, and after aiming it a few times and seeing how perfectly it fit in my purse, I was sold. "I'll take it. How much do I owe you?"

"It's already been paid for," Gia replied with a wink. She placed a box of bullets on the table and began packing up. "If you need anything else, don't be afraid to reach out..."

I made small talk with Gia for a few more minutes, discussing everything from guns to nail shops. She was cool as fuck and I could use a friend that had some ties to the game. As close as we were, after our argument last night, I knew there was no way in hell I could discuss my fears and worries with Yara because she didn't have an interest in my line of work. With plans to do some shopping and lunch the following week, I hugged Gia and waved goodbye to her and Hasani as they left out. Savion was sitting on the couch eyeing me when I turned back around. Gone was the playful demeanor he had seconds ago, replaced with an air of seriousness.

"Come have a seat next to me," he said, patting the spot on the sofa next to him.

I pointed to the door. "Actually, I was gonna head out before it got too—"

"Cashmere, come and have a seat," Savion repeated, and I could tell that it wasn't a request.

"Savion—"

"Cash...why do you suddenly need a gun for protection?" Savion asked, rising from his seat. He closed the space between us with three long strides. "And don't lie to me. Has that nigga been putting his hands on you?"

I balked at the statement. "Putting his hands on—no, Savion, I don't need a gun because I'm being abused. Lately I've been working this new job and I want to protect myself. The hours are really late so I feel better carrying some protection."

"If you're working late at night why isn't your man coming to pick you up?"

"Because I'm very capable of taking care of myself! I don't need a man to make sure I'm safe. I'm more than capable of doing it myself," I half shouted, faltering at the end because I became wrapped up in the Maison Margiela cologne Savion wore.

He peered down at me with thinly veiled anger. "What is it with you females? I swear all of you be up to the same stupid shit; latching on to a nigga that can't even get up off his ass and make sure his woman makes it home safe. Is that the relationship you're really standing in front of me defending?"

"Oh, so we're making blanket statements now?" I asked, cocking my head to the side. "That's what we're doing?"

"Now here comes the getting mad at having to hear the truth…"

"I'm not mad at hearing the truth! I'm mad at the fact that you're sitting here acting like…like…like—"

"Like what? The only real nigga you've ever come across?" Savion finished, leaning in so close our noses almost touched.

"No, like you're my fucking father, and since that nigga is dead, I don't need another one!"

Savion opened his mouth and I just knew he was getting ready to say some reckless shit when he grabbed me by the back of the head and pushed me into his awaiting lips. I instinctively pressed myself against him, moaning against his lips as his hand crept down my back and gave my ass a firm squeeze. All the anger and frustration I felt towards Savion was extinguished at the thought of how bad I was in need of some dick. Savion knew it; the cocky grin on his face as I wrapped my legs around his waist told him as much. He carried me down the hall to his bedroom without a single objection, his grin growing wider as I subconsciously adjusted myself on his waist.

"Who the fuck told you we were fucking?" I asked breathlessly, though the growing wetness between my legs betrayed me.

Savion stopped at the foot of his bed, a king-sized masterpiece that resided on another level of the room, looking down on its surroundings. He dropped me onto the thick black duvet, and replied, "You ain't say it yet, but by the time I'm done with you, you'll be begging for this dick."

I crab walked back into the center of the bed only to have Savion grab ahold of my ankles and tug me back towards him. The duvet hiked my dress up to my waist, revealing trembling thighs and silk red panties with a wet spot I couldn't explain away. Savion licked his lips at the sight, causing my cheeks to redden. His hands roamed up my thighs, each finger gently caressing my skin, until he reached my panties. He fingered the edges of the lace while I looked on, waiting for his next move. My heart nearly leapt out of my chest when he grabbed the fragile silk and ripped my panties clean off of me.

"Ya shit as fat as I thought it would be," Savion said before trailing his tongue down the slit of my pussy, lapping up its juices.

A smart remark died on my lips the moment he began making love to my pussy like it was an art form. I never expected a rough nigga like Savion to know a thing about eating pussy—maybe fucking the shit out it—but the way his tongue circled my clit before those juicy lips of his sucked on it proved me wrong in a good way. My legs started acting of their own volition, attempting to propel me away from Savion, but couldn't because of the viselike grip he had on them.

"Fuck you, Savion," I moaned as I grabbed the back of his head and busted one of the biggest nuts I had in a long time. "Fuck…fuck…"

My chest was heaving, my legs shaking, and I felt the room spin as I came down from the release. There was nothing better than an overdue orgasm and I could go for another, especially if it came at the hands of Savion. Speaking of Savion—

"Where are you going?" I asked Savion, who was halfway to the bedroom door.

He slipped out without a reply, leaving me lying there confused and hornier than ever. I fell back into the duvet with a whoosh and tried to figure out what I wanted. Vito was one of the few niggas to come into my life and take care of me without the need to throw it up in my face. Shit was tough between us right now, but was I really willing to throw away the time we had been together for someone else that I might not even have a future with?

"He had another bitch, a dead bitch to be specific, in your bed and you're really sitting here wondering if this is the right move to make?" I asked myself. I sat up and slid to the edge of the bed, shaking when my sensitive pussy shook with an after tremor. "Of course you are because like a dumbass, you can't fathom doing a nigga how he did you."

I had one foot firmly pressed on the floor when the door opened and in walked Savion with a tray of fruit and the unfinished bottle of Ciroc. One look at him reminded me of why I was willing to risk it all. He had stripped out of his clothes and wore nothing but a pair of boxers, giving me a good look at his eight-pack. Uncertainty flashed in Savion's eyes at catching me halfway off the bed.

"I want you to fuck me," I said, the words tumbling out of my mouth before I could take them back.

Savion didn't miss a beat. He placed the tray on a neighboring desk, took the bottle of Ciroc to the head long enough for three shots, and stalked over to me with a hungry look in his eyes. This time when we collided there was no more confusion. He pulled my dress over my head as I unclasped my bra with one hand and tugged his boxers down with the other.

"You sure about this?" Savion asked, giving me one last time to bow out before everything changed between us.

I turned around and crawled to the middle of the bed, making sure to give him a good view of what he was about to get, and made sure I was comfortable on the pillows before spreading my legs wide. Savion followed my lead, this time like a panther, his eyes never straying from mine. He hovered over me for a split second, studying every inch of my face as if he was making up his mind. After a few more seconds of decision making, he reached underneath his pillows and pulled out a box of condoms.

"Deadass?" I asked with my head tilted to the side.

Savion reached under the pillow on the other side of me and brandished a Glock. "I stay ready for whatever."

Only Savion could make me feel protected at a time he was supposed to be making me feel good all over. He placed the gun back underneath his pillow and returned his attention back to me. I watched in anticipation as he slid the condom over his dick. It was just as pretty as I remembered. I licked my lips in anticipation, wondering if it felt as good as it tasted. Savion entered me with no apologies, filling my walls with every last drop. If his head game didn't have me going crazy, then his stroke game had me ready to climb the walls.

"Whose is this?" Savion barked into my ear as he changed his tempo from lovemaking to straight fucking.

"Yours," I whispered into his ear as I came for the second time in a row.

Savion leaned in and whispered. "I don't give a fuck what you got going on with that nigga at home, but this pussy belongs to me now. You hear me?"

"Yes."

"Yes what?"

"Yes, Daddy."

Savion pressed his lips against mine with the same roughness he fucked me with, and came. He collapsed on top of me and laid there, his dick still inside of me pulsing. I stole a glance at him from the corner of my eye. He was nearly asleep. I couldn't even be mad because good pussy did that to you. We laid like that or a while, with me running my hands through his hair as he planted gentle kisses on my neck, until my stomach emitted a growl. Savion's eyes popped open in surprise while mine snapped shut out of embarrassment.

"You really tryna play sleep like that loud ass growl ain't come from your stomach?" he laughed.

I fake snored real loud for added measure.

"Aight, I'll see what I got in the fridge."

Savion disappeared with a peck on the lips, leaving me cold without his body on mine. I rolled onto my side, patiently waiting to regain the use of my legs. Savion had flipped me all over this bed and bent me into positions I couldn't even make sense of. I was still smiling to myself when I heard a buzzing by the foot of the bed. A few rolls later, I was at the end of the bed staring at my purse. I considered letting it ring, then I remembered that I had plenty of clients that could be calling to place an order. Grabbing my purse, I scurried into the bathroom and picked up without looking at the caller ID.

"Hello?" I asked as I crept over to the cracked bathroom window. I opened it all the way and leaned out to keep Savion from hearing anything.

"Cash, it's me; Wale."

My heart skipped a beat. Wale was Vito's brother and a local dealer that had connections all around the city. I asked him if he could get me a meeting with his connect, who was a mysterious nigga that was picky when it came to working with new clients. This call came right on time because I was in desperate need of some product.

"Wale, please tell me you got me the meeting."

"Yeah, this nigga wants to meet you right now. Where you at so I can come through and grab you."

"Right now? I exclaimed. In a lower voice I replied, "Does it have to be right now? I'm kind of in the middle of something."

"Cash, what did I tell you when you asked for this meeting?"

"That it could happen at any time."

"Exactly. This nigga wants to meet you at six o'clock on the dot and if you ain't there then you can kiss your meeting goodbye."

"Six o'clock? It's five-fifteen. Is he deadass serious right now?"

"It only takes twenty minutes to get to his spot. Ten if I really push it."

"Where's his spot at? I can meet you there."

"I can't tell you that."

I banged my head against the windowsill. "Of course you can't. Fine, I'll meet you at your apartment in twenty minutes."

"Cash, you're cutting it close."

"I know," I replied. As I hurried over to the Savion's glass paneled shower, I stepped inside and started pressing buttons, praying one would just give me water. "We'll make it there in time, trust me."

Ice-cold water came shooting from the ceiling, scaring me half to death and waking me up all at the same damn time. I threw my burner phone to the side where it couldn't get wet and then focused on finding the hot water. A few button presses later I was doused in hot water. For five minutes I took one of the most vigorous hoe baths of my life and sprang out of the shower in record time. My hair, which was nothing more than a fluffy mass by now, would have to stay that way. I toweled off and was halfway to the bathroom door when I remembered my burner phone sitting on the floor.

"I can't leave without—Savion! You scared the shit out of me!"

Savion was standing in the doorway of the bathroom as soon as I opened the door. He wore an amused grin until he spotted the phone in my hand. The grin dropped and he stepped aside. I already knew what he was thinking, and if I had the time to convince him otherwise, I would. It would simply have to wait.

"I was knocking to let you know that I was heating up some lasagna I made last night, but I got a feeling you're not staying."

I had my dress around my neck and was clasping my bra while trying to slip one foot into my shoes. "Nope, an emergency came up and I gotta go."

"Or your man called."

"Savion, it's not even like that. A friend of mine called me saying she needs my help with a situation, and she rarely calls looking for help so I have to look out for her." I rummaged through my purse and came up with a scrunchie. "Aha!"

Savion watched with thinly veiled interest as I managed to take my wild wet fro and transform it into a messy high bun. He shrugged nonchalantly. "Aight, look out for your girl. I'll see you around."

"I promise to make this up to you," I said, pecking him on the lips and hurrying out of his bedroom, checking my watch along the way.

Ten minutes. I managed to get out of Savion's place in ten minutes, which left me with ten minutes to be at Wale's place. God was looking out for me big time because traffic was light on this side of Brooklyn. I skidded to a stop in front of Wale's place where he was on the stoop with his niggas. They all eyed the brand new Benz wearily until I rolled my window down and shouted for Wale to get in.

"This bitch is bad, Cash. Where the fuck you get the money for this from?" he asked, fingering the fine grain leather covering the dashboard.

"I've been busy. Now gimme the address so we can hurry up and make it to this guy. We got…shit, fifteen minutes."

Wale rattled off the address to a lounge nearly on the other side of town. The only way I was making it there in fifteen minutes was if I ran every red light I came across, and that was if there was no traffic. That didn't mean I wouldn't at least try.

"Cash, I spoke to my brother about you putting him rehab, an expensive one at that."

"You think I would put him in one of those shitty ones where he wouldn't get the help he needs? Vito's always looked out for me. I wouldn't do him like that."

Wale bit his lip as if he was trying to figure out how to ask the obvious question that was on his mind. After another minute, he blurted out, "Cash, you selling?"

"Why else would I be trying to get a meeting with a supplier, Wale? It damn sure ain't to share tips and tricks. I unloaded the coke Vito had, and now I need some more."

"So why not go to his old supplier?"

I reached my first red light, looked both ways, and slid right through it. "Because that nigga cut Vito off after we paid off his debt the last time. He hasn't been able to find one since then."

"So how'd he get coke?"

"I was hoping you could tell me that. Vito tells you everything."

Wale sighed. "That was before he started dabbling again. I told him to leave that shit alone before he fucked around and overdosed, and he took that as me being jealous because I could never move weight like him. His call from rehab was the first one I received in a while. If he got coke from someone, the only person that knows is him."

"So then where the fuck did those two kilos come from?"

"Two kilos? You moved two kilos? Alone?" Wale looked nothing short of impressed. "How long did it take?"

"Like three weeks since it was me by myself."

Wale let out a low whistle. "Damn, sis. That's a come up."

"Nah, bro; just hustling."

I pulled up to C'est Magnifique Lounge and Bar at six on the dot. Wale could barely keep up with me as I skipped the entire line and headed straight inside at the mention of my name. It was still a little slow with the dinner crowd slowly funneling in. I looked around the room and spotted an older man sitting by himself. The dim lighting of the lounge wasn't enough to hide the diamond pinky ring to his left finger and the tailored Armani suit he wore. I barely took two steps towards him when I bumped into a handsome man dressed in a janitor's uniform.

"My bad, ma," he said, holding me by the waist until I steadied myself.

I flashed him a surprised smile. "It's okay. I wasn't looking where I was going."

"Can I make it up to you by buying you a drink?"

I took one good look at this fine ass man—with his flawless

chocolate skin, brown doe eyes, full lips, and waves spinning just how I liked them—and tried to figure out why I couldn't have met him at least ten minutes later. "I'm sorry"—I checked out the name on his uniform—"Ahmad. As tempting as a drink sounds, I can't. I have an important meeting with someone right now."

"I understand. Well, maybe I'll see you around sometime," he said with a smile and kept it moving towards the back of the club.

I made a beeline for the table of my supplier and sat across from him. "I know I'm really late, but there was an issue with traffic—"

"Who are you?" he demanded, giving me an *are you crazy?* look. "I'm here waiting on my wife."

"Oh, I'm sorry. I thought you were someone else," I apologized, rising from the chair. I walked over to Wale, who was standing by the entrance, and slapped him on the arm. "Why didn't you stop me from going over to that man and making a fool of myself?"

"I figured it would lessen the blow of what I'm getting ready to tell you. My supplier said it's a no-go."

I frantically looked around the club. "What? When did you speak to him?"

"It's not important, Cash. He said no."

"Why? Because I was a few minutes late? Call him on the phone, Wale, and tell him I promise I'll never be late again."

Wale placed his hands on either side of my shoulders. "Cash, once the man says no, then it's no. I can ask around and see if someone else has product."

"Will it be the best? You told me this nigga deals with the best."

"It won't be top notch, but it should be good enough to give your clients for the time being—"

I placed my hands on Wale's cheeks, and replied, "If I'm going to create my empire then I need the best. I'm out here selling to the elite so I need elite shit. Now please, Wale, get on the phone and tell him I need another meeting. Shit, I'll sleep in front of this club just to make sure I'm on time."

"I'm sorry, Cash. How about we grab a drink and I'll help you come up with your next move?"

"Fine."

I followed Wale over to the bar and took a seat, ready to pour out my troubles. While he sipped on something smooth like a glass of Crown Royale on the rocks, I opted for some shots of Jack Daniels honey whiskey. I was on my third one when I spotted something interesting. The janitor, Ahmad, was talking to one of the waitresses. It wasn't a normal conversation either; whatever he was telling her she was obediently nodding her head to. I've never in my life seen a waitress stare at a janitor that way, like her life was on the line; like if she didn't follow the directions she was given, it would be lights out for her.

"Wale?"

"Hmm?" Wale replied over the rim of his glass.

"You wouldn't call the supplier back not because he would say no, but because you never called him in the first place. He's been here all along, hasn't he?"

"Cash—"

It was too late; I was already out of my seat and stalking towards Ahmad, who was carrying a bucket into the back of the club. I caught the door just in time, sliding right between it and tapping Ahmad on the shoulder. His eyes widened in shock at the sight of me.

"Yo, ma, you can't be back here. It's for employees only, and if the owner catches you back here—"

"I shouldn't get into too much trouble because you're the owner, aren't you?" I gave him a more thorough once over and caught another sign that I was barking up the right tree. "I'm not saying that janitors don't make bread, but I don't know too many who work in $3,000 Berluti oxfords. I know who you are, and all I'm asking for is a second chance."

The shock Ahmad wore disappeared at the mention of us doing business. In a menacing tone, he replied, "Look, I already told Wale the answer is no. I expect punctuality from anyone I'm doing business with."

"No disrespect, but you didn't leave me too much time to get here. Do you know how many parking tickets I'm probably gonna get in the mail speeding to get here? I'm serious as fuck about doing business with you." I didn't realize how much this opportunity meant to me until I dropped down on my knees and grabbed Ahmad's hand, giving the pinky ring on his hand a kiss. "If you give me one more shot to impress you I swear you won't regret it. I put that on my life."

Ahmad stared down at me, thinking long and hard, before replying, "Come up off the floor before someone sees us and gets the wrong idea." I scrambled hastily to my feet and followed him down the hall. "I run a tight ship: I don't tolerate lateness, short payments, and if you're looking for someone to hit with excuses, I'm not the one."

"Never that."

We entered an office at the end of the hall. It was snug, fitting a few cabinets, a desk, and a few chairs. Ahmad sat at the edge of the desk and welcomed me to one of the two chairs in front of it. I sat in the farthest one to prevent anyone from getting the wrong idea.

"You wanna know why I'm giving you this second chance? Because when I asked you if you wanted to have a drink, you declined and instead you remained humble while trying to handle business. That was your only saving grace," Ahmad said without his eyes leaving mine. He held his hand out to me. "Once we shake there's no going back. You ready to get this money?"

I grabbed Ahmad's hand without hesitation. "Get it? It's always been mine, I just need to put some weight behind it."

Yara

It was a little past noon when I arrived home. My head was bumping, I could barely stay awake in my Uber, and no matter how much water I drunk it wasn't enough. I was sure as shit that I looked ugly too; my hair was all over the place underneath the hat I borrowed from Cash, and I made the mistake of falling asleep without taking off my makeup. *Oh well, if a nigga can't see you in your true form and accept it, then he's not the man for you,* I thought on my trek upstairs to Quade's apartment. Of course I was talking all that shit before entering, but once I was inside I poked my head down the hall, silently hoping Quade was out handling business. My heart leapt for joy until I heard him talking in the bedroom. I crept down the hall, careful not to make too much noise.

"…What's Amaya up to?" I heard him ask as he fingered the blue duvet covering a four-poster bed fit for a king.

I felt my blood boil at another woman's name coming out of his mouth. After everything I had been through with Amir, there was no way in hell I was getting ready to be under the roof of another cheating bastard. I wasn't sure who this Amaya was, but if that's who he wanted, then I could pack all my shit and move right back to the hotel I was in.

Those were the exact words that were poised to fly out of my mouth until Quade added, "Yeah, she's beautiful, but she's no Yara." He laughed. "Nigga, shut up. Of course I ain't never gon' say another female look better than my girl. Even if she did, she still doesn't, because she ain't my girl. Point blank simple. Now tell me what Amaya's been up to 'cause I'm tryna have this business handled by next week. I'm thinking about taking Yara on a nice vacation since Jamaica ain't work out too well."

My heart melted at the affectionate tone Quade used to talk about me. It was a far cry from the blatant disinterest he had when we first met. I was so touched by his words that of course my stupid ass had to exclaim, "Awww."

Quade turned around with the quickness, reaching for his Glock along the way. This was the second time within a few weeks that I had been staring down the end of his barrel, and I was waiting for the day when it got old.

"You stay strapped even in the house?" I asked in surprise.

"Zeus, lemme call you back; Yara just came in." Quade hung up his phone and tossed it on the bed along with the gun. "How the fuck you snuck up on me I'll never know, but I bet you won't do that again."

"Nah, I will; I gotta make sure you stay sharp. Who knows, you might rub off on me and I'll start carrying a piece of my own," I joked, closing the space between us and placing my head on his chest.

Yes, I talked a good game until I smelled his cologne mixed with the scent of fresh laundry detergent, something he knew I was a sucker for. Quade's hand reached down and stroked my cheek, making me feel warm all over. At least that's what I thought he was doing until he did it again, except this time a bit firmer.

"What happened to your face?"

I rolled my eyes. "It's a long story. I'd rather tell you over breakfast."

"No, you gon' tell me right now, or else."

"Or else what?"

"Or else I'mma go to that club and get the answers myself."

I thought of the last time Quade was at a club, and relented. "I got into a fight with some bitch that had a problem with Cash. I had been drinking tequila and it puts me in a fighting mood. I went for the girl before she could get to my girl."

"And then?"

I knew if I told Quade about one of those men placing a gun to my head that would be it for everyone, so I decided to keep that part to myself. "And then Cash helped me beat the hoe up. We went back to her place where I slept off most of this hangover. Now all I need is a shower along with a hot meal so I can get rid of the rest."

"You must be fucked up if you walked past all that furniture without noticing it."

Furniture?

Quade grabbed my hand and led me back to the front of the apartment, which was fully furnished. The living room had a set of blue sofas that were similar to the ones I had at Amir's place. A 52" TV sat opposite the sofa with an intricate wall unit flanking it. I glanced closer and saw that on each of the shelves were the pictures I had in my keepsake box, as well as pictures I had back at my place with Amir. Quade was like a sour patch kid; as easily as you wanted to kill him, he could make you wanna hug him tight and never let go. That was exactly how I felt as I wrapped my arms around his neck, nuzzling into him with all my might.

"You did an amazing job," I said, pecking him on the cheek. "How did you get all of this furniture here so quick? I was only gone for twelve, fourteen hours tops."

"You don't need to worry about that, just know that your man wanted you to come home to a home," Quade assured me. He glanced around the apartment, and thought out loud, "It sure is a lot of shit in here now. I don't know how y'all do this. Nigga at the furniture store told me I was a minimalist, whatever that means..."

Quade continued my tour of the apartment, which now had a full dining area, a kitchen stocked with everything a cook like myself would need, and ended in the bedroom. Apparently I had interrupted Quade while he was dressing the bed. I admired the vanity, which was set up with all of my lotions and perfumes. Quade stood posted up against the bed, watching and waiting for me to say something.

"This is one of the kindest things anyone has ever done for me," I told Quade. "I know how hard it must've been to give up so much of your space for me."

Quade's expression became unreadable, but he replied, "If I got it then it's yours."

And like that, Quade proved his loyalty to me once again.

My heart swelled with affection at such a simple declaration. I knew right then and there I had to get him out of the house so I could carry out some plans of my own.

"I'm starving? Are you starving?"

"As a matter of fact, ever since I started eating all this healthy shit I'm hungry all the time...what you wanna eat?"

I thought of something far enough that I would have time to get ready, but close enough where the food wouldn't get cold. "There's a diner right by Broadway Junction that makes some really good breakfast. I'll take their deluxe breakfast."

"I think I know the spot you're talking about. Paphos or some shit like that..." Quade replied, leaning off of the bed and making a beeline for the door. "I'll be back."

I stood there playing it cool, but once the front door opened and shut, I went straight to work. With a slice of bread in my belly, I popped a couple of Tylenols and made a beeline for the bathroom. I primped, plucked, shaved, and exfoliated every part of my body while jamming to Lil Kim's "Big Momma Thang." It was the only way I could hype myself up for what was getting ready to come. I barely finished slipping into one of the teddies I had purchased from Victoria's Secret when I heard the front door open. I hopped on the bed and laid across it all casual, like I wasn't scared out of my ass.

"I forgot to ask what kind of sausage you wanted so I got pork and turk—oh shit. I guess you want a completely different sausage," Quade said at the sight of me lying there with my booty out.

My heart was banging against my chest as I seductively crawled over to him with my best "I wanna fuck you" face, but I wasn't gonna back down this time. If I could trust Quade with my heart, then it was time I trusted him with my body.

198

"The other day you told me you like to fuck on some vanilla shit. Now you're dressed like you're ready to get the D and then some," Quade said, his brows lifting as I sat on my haunches, giving him a better view of the teddy. "Are you sure about this, Yara?"

"I wouldn't be sitting here in front of you if I wasn't ready, now would I?"

Quade grabbed me by the neck and shoved his tongue roughly down my throat. I panicked, grabbing his shoulders as if to stop him from choking me when the craziest thing happened.

"See, I knew you wasn't ready," Quade said with a chuckle as he sauntered over to the desk in the corner of the room and began removing the containers from the bag.

I rolled to the other side of the bed, jumped off, and shoved him into the wall. For the second time today, I caught him by surprise. I grabbed one of his hands and led it slowly down my stomach until it reached the soaking wet crotch of the teddy. Quade reached into his pocket and pulled out a switchblade. It sprang open with a flick of his wrist. He laughed at the fear in my eyes.

"You still trust me?"

I nodded.

"Good, then you'll know all I want do is take this off of you," he replied, running the blade gently down the front of the teddy.

With one upwards flick of his wrist, it was ripped clean down the middle, freeing my breasts and giving him a peekaboo view of my pussy. He deftly closed the switchblade and tossed it on the desk without taking his eyes off of me. I shivered underneath his touch, which was cool on my feverish skin. His fingers traced light circles over my collarbone, pinched my aching nipples, combed over my hips until gripping my ass. Quade pressed me against him, giving me a feeling of his dick against my leg.

"You like that?" he asked huskily.

I nodded again. "Yes."

Quade's hands grabbed the teddy and gave it a rough tug. The sound of shredding fabric filled the silent room. The straps dug into my shoulders for a split second before disappearing, replaced by Quade's hands massaging them as he backed me towards the bed. He picked me up and laid me down gently, which was a stark contrast to how he had been handling me before. I closed my eyes in anticipation, ready for whatever Quade had ready for me. Musiq Soulchild's "Whoknows" filled the room, reminding me of how monumental right now was. I opened my eyes and there was Quade, hovering above me with an unreadable expression on his face.

"What? Are you having second thoughts?" I asked jokingly, cocking my head to the side.

Quade shook his head. "Nah, I just got this weird ass feeling in my stomach. I don't think I should've snuck that Popeye's biscuit on the way home…"

"Or…maybe you're nervous?"

He shook his head. "Nah, I ain't been nervous since '95."

I wanted to ask what happened in 1995, but was distracted by Quade spreading my legs and peppering the insides of my thighs with gentle kisses. My legs trembled as he grew closer to my soaking wet center, each kiss involving a little tongue to give me a good idea of what was to come. However, when Quade's tongue made love to my clit, everything negative I ever felt about sex evaporated from my mind as a strong orgasm seized me.

"What happened to 'I don't like nobody eating my pussy'? Hmm?" Quade asked with each kiss he trailed up my stomach.

He reached my nipples and greeted each one with a swirl and suck of his tongue. *Since when are my nipples this sensitive?* I thought as I arched my back to bring them closer to him. It was like Quade flipped a switch somewhere deep inside of me, and my body belonged to him. His lips pressed against mine possessively. I could taste my juices on his tongue, and could feel another ocean developing between my legs. Quade noticed when his free hand went down and fingered me.

"Shut up," I retorted with a bite to his shoulder.

"Since you talking all that shit, I got something to calm that ass down," Quade replied with a devilish grin that should never touch such an innocent looking face.

He sat up for a second to strap up and laid down ready to get it in. I let out a breath I wasn't even aware I was holding when he positioned himself between my legs. *At least he's letting me keep something familiar,* I thought as he eased into me gently. I wrapped my arms around his neck and closed my eyes, feeling myself slip back into that sense of familiarity. Just when I felt myself relaxing, gravity changed gears, and all of a sudden I was on top with Quade looking up at me.

"Both you and I know I have no idea how to ride," I said, feeling my cheeks heat up with embarrassment; I knew I had to be the most inexperienced woman he had ever dealt with. "You know what? You were right, I'm not ready—"

Quade sat up easily and placed his hands on my hips. "Stop selling yourself short. You think I just woke up one day and knew how to handle niggas the way I do? Anything you want in life will take some practice. Trust me on that. You know those big ass exercise balls they have at the gym? Imagine you're on one of those…"

I followed Quade's instructions the best I could, and after a few minutes of moving without his laughing in my face, I felt enough courage to take it to the next level. I pushed him back down, placed my hands on his chest, and recalled the way Anika rode Amir. I emulated it the best I could, bouncing up and down on Quade's dick like it was another day at the gym. A firm slap on the ass knocked me right from the gym and back to the bedroom where Quade was staring up at me, biting his lip as I took him to unexpected heights. His hands crept up my waist until they wrapped around my throat, squeezing it gently at first.

"You like that?" he barked.

I picked up the pace as I felt myself getting ready to cum again. "Yes, Daddy. Choke me harder."

Quade cut off my air supply completely. I had to rely on the last breath I had taken, and with each passing second I felt a high like no other. My pussy contracted on Quade's dick before I felt myself cum harder than I ever had in my life. His hands disappeared from around my neck, allowing me to fall into a heap bedside him. I lay there, chest heaving, body sweating, pussy twitching, with a big ass grin on my face.

Quade moved the mess of hair covering my face and gave me a peck on the lips. "You good?"

All I could do was give him a weak ass nod before closing my eyes and resting. The movement was slight, but I felt Quade disappear because his warmth left with him. I dozed for a few, only waking up as I felt Quade clean me with a warm towel. Somehow I managed to curl up at the head of the bed, still biting my lower lip as I replayed everything over. My daydreaming was interrupted by a glass of orange juice being placed to my lips. I drank the entire cup in five gulps.

"Hungry?"

I shook my head.

"Nah, you gotta eat something before round two."

My eyes snapped open in surprise. "Round two?"

Quade laughed at the sight. "I'mma need some more of that before the day is over. So you need to sit up and eat some of this breakfast."

At the mention of being blessed again, I found enough strength to sit up a little higher and enjoy my food. Once we were stuffed, we laid in bed talking, and not any of those regular conversations people had. I shouldn't have expected anything different from Quade, who had proved on more than one occasion that he was crazy.

"But if time travel doesn't exist then explain that picture of the nigga that looks just like Jay Z from nearly a hundred years ago? Explain it, Yara," Quade said, pounding his fist into his hand for emphasis.

I shook with silent laughter at his passion. "Photoshop maybe?"

"Nah, next thing you know, you'll start telling me you don't believe in aliens." My silence was enough of a confirmation. "Yara, you can't be serious right now. Deadass?"

"Quade, aliens don't exist."

"So then what are they hiding at Area 51?"

Quade's phone buzzing on the nightstand kept me from admitting that I had no idea what they kept at Area 51. I sat quietly, not wanting to be a distraction while he handled business. Gone was the playful Quade, replaced by someone far more serious.

"You found him? Are you positive? You think you can keep that nigga high until I get there?" Quade asked, hopping out of bed and disappearing into the bathroom.

The shower turned on, drowning out the rest of the conversation. Quade emerged twenty minutes later fully dressed in his signature sweats with a hoodie and vest, thanks to the cool night air. He ended his conversation at the sight of me sitting there watching him, waiting for some type of explanation.

"Remember the niggas that stole from me? Well I found the last one, and I need to get to him before he disappears," Quade explained.

"How long will you be gone?"

"A couple hours. I'll call you when I'm on my way home."

He disappeared from the room like a shadow, only to return a few seconds later. He planted a kiss on my lips, and said, "By the time I come back you better have a good explanation for why you don't believe in aliens."

I rolled my eyes. "I will."

Without Quade, the energy in the room wasn't the same. The laughter we shared was replaced by the silence of me missing him, and he hadn't even been gone a full five minutes. In the span of two days I had developed a stronger bond with Quade than I had with Amir over the past two years. It was too soon to admit out loud, but I knew deep down on the inside I was falling in love with him.

Quade

It was going on eight when I arrived in Baltimore City. Today the block was eerily quiet; there was no one posted up in front of the corner stores or the many vacant houses that lined each block, with a few brand new homes peppered in between. However, I knew better than to think that empty streets meant no heat. I made sure to use one of my burner cars in the event that something popped off. Honestly, I should've brought backup, but I had a few niggas out here I kept on payroll to make sure I could come through whenever I needed to, including my cousin, Wootie. He was standing outside smoking on a loosie when I pulled up.

"Wassup, baby," Wootie greeted with that thick Baltimore twang.

I dapped him up. "Wassup, my nigga. You said he in there?"

"We told him that we needed testers for some new shit we just got in and he been smoking it all day. Better catch that bitch before he overdose," Wootie replied between pulls.

"How many bodies in there?"

"It's a full house, but the nigga you looking for is on the first floor."

"Aight, make sure no one comes in."

I approached the abandoned house with my piece on my side, ready to press the fuck out of this nigga and get back home to my girl. I had spent the entire ride thinking of Yara, from the touch of her skin to the way she always smelled like lavender and vanilla. Those memories died the moment I set foot across the threshold of the house. It was silent, save for the occasional creak of the wood overhead paired with coughing fits. Deeper into the house I began to hear rumblings of human life. I entered what was once the living room with my gun ready to end anything that stood in my way. There, sitting with a small pile of crack vials by his side, was J Reed. He was knocked out cold with some bitch sitting next to him sparking up her next hit. Another nigga lay passed out on the floor, a cough escaping his chapped lips every few seconds.

"Move," I commanded the woman with a wave of my gun.

She picked up as many of the unused vials as she could and moved to the other side of the room with the man, who hadn't woken up at the commotion. I kicked his leg, waking him instantly. He started mumbling under his breath and looking around for his pipe like a true fiend. I turned on the light from my iPhone, steadying it on his dumbass.

"Ay, look up at me," I barked with another firm kick.

J Reed placed his hands in the air. "Yo, who the fuck is that?"

"Who the fuck do you think it is? After stealing my shit you thought I wouldn't catch up to any of you niggas?"

"What shit? I ain't steal nothing, I swear!" J Reed exclaimed, shielding his eyes from the light.

"So you, Big Boy, Kenny, and Jerry ain't rob my nigga two weeks ago? Huh?" I asked, bending down and smacking that nigga across the face with my Glock in a moment of frustration. "Now I know full and well none of you niggas are smart enough to set up a plan that smooth to rob me, so I wanna know who put y'all up to it."

"I didn't have nothing to do with that robbery!"

I pinned him to the wall with my foot, pressing it into his neck to keep him in place. "My lieutenant told me it was four niggas that robbed him. If you wasn't there with your niggas, then who was?"

"Kenny's cousin. I wasn't feeling to well so Kenny got his cousin to step in for me. He's the one that got a cut of the ten keys. Kenny looked out and gave me a little something, but it definitely wasn't nothing more than once."

"What's his cousin's name?"

"Derico...Dan Rico...Danny Devito...it's Davito. His cousin's name is Davito."

I dug my sneaker deeper into his neck. "Where can I find him?"

"I don't know, Quade. Ever since I got on this shit real bad them niggas stopped fucking with me. The only reason why they let me in on that last lick was because I promised them I would use the money to get clean. As you can see, I broke that promise."

"If you don't know that, then at least tell me you know who the fuck put y'all up to it. Who set up the plan, J Reed?"

J Reed croaked, "All I heard from Kenny was that some Miami niggas approached him with a job, saying that if he pulled it off he could walk away with a lot of money. He had this schedule of the drops y'all made and gave it to Kenny, who made the plan and gave each of us a part. He never mentioned their names just that they came from

Miami."

"Why the coke? Why not the coke and the money? And what the fuck would they gain from stealing my shit other than pissing me off?"

J Reed shrugged. "I don't know, fam. Maybe they just wanted your shit off the street to make room for their own."

"Ain't no new shit on the streets."

"Yet," J Reed choked out.

"What?" I snapped, busting him in the head once again.

"I mean they shit ain't on the street yet 'cause I'm sure they probably tryna squeeze y'all out. But them niggas wild as fuck for coming for any of you Townsend Brothers. To be honest, that's one of the reasons why I ain't take part in the stickup; I don't want those problems."

"Smart choice," I replied, staring down at him deciding whether or not I wanted to kill his simple ass.

I grew up with J Reed and it was nothing short of surprising that he became a crackhead. His moms was the elementary school nurse and she would always patch up my knees after I got into a fight with the kids that bullied me. Never once did she treat me different like the adults did. Sometimes she even gave me a lollipop and let me hang with her in the nurse's office until my mother got to the school to pick me up. This nigga was breaking his mother's heart all by himself; I wouldn't be responsible for putting one final dent in it.

"You not gon' kill me?" J Reed asked, genuinely surprised.

I removed my foot from his throat. "Not today. Do yourself a favor and get off this shit before you kill your damn self."

I know I was the last motherfucker that needed to tell someone to get clean, but maybe he needed to hear it from someone that didn't give a fuck about him. Tugging my hoodie lower on my face, I backed up and exited out of the room. I was halfway to the door when I heard it. The same floorboard that squeaked on my way in. An arm wrapped around my throat before I could react, trapping me in place. For a second I thought it was J Reed, but the sleeves of his jacket matched the same man that was passed out on the floor seconds ago.

"You niggas set me up," I hissed as I planted my feet so I could flip this nigga on his back.

A hot chuckle heated up my cheek, followed by the reply, "You think I would work with some fucking crackheads? No, nigga, I just knew you would come looking for J Reed in order to get some answers. I already told you that you'd know who the fuck I am when I'm ready for you to."

I was more than positive this nigga was looking for a long ass conversation where he could tell me about the numerous times he outsmarted me, but I didn't have a listening ear to lend. I elbowed him in his stomach, forcing him to let go with a grunt. He reacted quicker than I expected, lunging into me and sending us crashing to the walls. The sound of tearing wallpaper echoed through the hall as plaster sprinkled everywhere. I hit him with two uppercuts and went for a third when I felt this strange stinging sensation. Somewhere in the midst of our fighting, this nigga pulled out a blade and stabbed me.

"What the fuck is going on?"

J Reed appeared in the doorway along with the girl that was with him. That split second gave me enough time to put a bullet in that nigga's head. He crumpled to the floor in a heap, his hood falling off to reveal an unfamiliar face. Wootie came busting through the door with a couple of his niggas flanking him.

"Yo, where the fuck did this nigga come from?" he asked, staring from me to J Reed to the body on the floor.

"He was in here pretending to be a crackhead," I said, bending down and patting his pockets. I didn't get a wallet, but I did get some car keys. "Have some of your niggas ride around looking for this car. I want everything inside of it. I don't care if it's a stick of gum. I wanna know who the fuck this nigga is and where he came from."

Sheer terror spread across Wootie's face as he took in the tear in my jacket where I was stabbed. "He got one off on you? Yo, you want me to take you to the hospital?"

"Nah, that nigga poked me but I'm good. It's just a little nick," I said, showing him the slash on my side from where the knife sliced a little meat. "I need you to get rid of this body while I head to the pharmacy to get something to sew this up with."

"Nah, I think you need to go to the hospital. Johns Hopkins ain't too far. Can you really stich yourself up?"

"It wouldn't be the first time."

The block was stirring after those shots went off. It was only a matter of time before the cops came looking around for the source of the drama. I hopped into my car and peeled off with the nearest gas station in mind. My hopes were squashed when I recalled that this wasn't home where I could easily run into a million 24 hour Duane Reade's or a bodega on every block. I had no choice but to head to the hospital. I was halfway there when a wave of dizziness washed over me.

"What the fuck?" I said to myself as I felt my abdomen.

With the adrenaline from my fight out of my system, I could feel the cramping of my stomach. I reached underneath my hoodie and felt a deep gash across my stomach. I was bleeding out in the middle of the road with no hospital in sight. There was only one person I could call on during a time like this. Her beautiful face lit up my screen as our FaceTime connected.

"Are you on your way home?" Yara asked with a bright smile.

"Nah, I don't think I'mma make it," I admitted.

Yara's smile dropped instantly. "Quade, what's wrong with you? You don't look too good."

"None of that is important. All I want is for your face to be the last thing I ever see."

"Quade!" Yara screamed, but it was too late.

My vision blurred for a split second at the same time I went flying through the intersection, colliding with a car. Yara's screams were overpowered by the sounds of metal hitting metal, glass spraying the night air, and the feeling of my lungs taking their last few breaths before everything went black.

TO BE CONTINUED...

ALSO BY TYA MARIE

A Brooklyn Love Affair: Vixen & Gino's Story

A Brooklyn Love Affair 2: Vixen & Gino's Story

A Brooklyn Love Affair 3: Vixen & Gino's Story

A Brooklyn Love Affair 4: Vixen & Gino's Story

Never Should've Loved a Thug

Never Should've Loved Another Thug

The Heart of a King: In Love with a Savage

The Heart of a King 2: In Love with a Savage

Grimey: Married to the King of Miami

Grimey 2: Married to the King of Miami

Ain't Nothing like a Real One: Faded Off an Inked God

Ain't Nothing like a Real One 2: Faded Off an Inked God

Chosen By The King of Miami: A Grimey Love Affair

Chosen By The King of Miami 2: A Grimey Love Affair

CONNECT WITH TYA MARIE

Facebook: *Authoress Tya Marie*

Instagram: *Tya_Marie1028*

Twitter: *LaTya_Marie*

Facebook Group: *Tea with Tya Marie*

Looking for a publishing home?

Royalty Publishing House, Where the Royals reside, is accepting submissions for writers in the urban fiction genre. If you're interested, submit the first 3-4 chapters with your synopsis to submissions@royaltypublishinghouse.com.

Check out our website for more information:

www.royaltypublishinghouse.com.

Text ROYALTY to 42828 to join our mailing list!

To submit a manuscript for our review, email us at submissions@royaltypublishinghouse.com

Text RPHCHRISTIAN to 22828 for our CHRISTIAN ROMANCE novels!

Text RPHROMANCE to 22828 for our INTERRACIAL ROMANCE novels!

CPSIA information can be obtained
at www.ICGtesting.com
Printed in the USA
LVOW13s1935140218
566611LV00018B/451/P